HOW TORIE GOT HER HEX BACK

M.J. CAAN

Vinci

BOOKS

By M.J. Caan

Singing Falls Witches

Vinci Books

vinci-books.com

Published by Vinci Books Ltd in 2025

1

A CIP catalogue record for this book is available from the British Library.
Paperback ISBN: 9781036705596
The EU GPSR authorised representative is Logos Europe, 9 rue Nicolas Poussion, 17000 La Rochelle, France contact@logoseurope.eu

Chapter One

Torie sat cross-legged on the floor, staring at the fireplace. Then she looked over at the pieces of wood she had brought in, which were stacked next to an old newspaper.

"How the hell do you even make a fire?" she wondered to herself. In her previous life as a married woman, she made fire by pressing a button, and watching the gas ignite the crystals in her modern style fireplace. But how do people actually do it with sticks and paper?

Just a week ago, she would have issued a mental command that would have caused the wood to ignite, filling the living room with warmth and light. But that was before.

Before she sacrificed her powers to save the newborn baby of her ex-husband's fae mistress.

Now, she was forced with the seemingly impossible task of replicating the first thing early man created in order to survive: fire.

She sighed, reached for the newspaper and crumpled it, creating a bed in the fireplace. Now, do you light it and then put the wood on top, or put the wood on, then light it? It made more sense to do the former in her mind, but that didn't mean it would work. She only had one newspaper, and therefore, only one shot.

In the end, she decided to stack the pieces of wood on top first and weave more crumbled pieces of paper between the logs.

Satisfied with what she saw, she reached for the starter lying on the mantle and lit the paper. Slowly, the fire she created made its way between the logs, lighting them as it went.

Pleased with herself, Torie smiled and made her way to her feet. Her knees had progressed from creaking to giving slight pops that were echoed by the sharp exhales of breath as she stood. The floor was now her enemy; along with the ottoman, the couch in the spare room upstairs that was way too deep.

She made a mental note to check out the only gym in town later in the week. With the coming cooler air, her joints were already starting to protest, beginning when she swung her legs out of bed in the mornings and not letting up until she made her way back into said bed that night.

Why hadn't she tried to magically fix that when she still had her powers?

"You know why, Torie. Because you had no reason to think you'd ever lose your magic."

She made her way to the kitchen and poured herself a shot of whiskey to sip. She could have waited until Elric had come by and asked him to make her a fire, but wasn't that something, along with bathing and feeding herself, that she should be able to do on her own? Besides, she liked having a fire. The crackle was soothing in the ever-present silence of the house.

Had it always been so quiet? She tried not to think

about her mother. That path would take her someplace dark, and that was the last thing she needed. No, she needed to put on her happy face. Her friends would be coming by later to check in on her, and she had to convince them she was alright.

Food.

That was what she needed to focus on now. Put out a spread so they would see she was in a good place.

Except that she wasn't. The thought of taking out pans, prepping food, baking and sautéing...all things that she truly loved, was exhausting. Instead, she went to the pantry, retrieved some mixed nuts and tossed them into a large service bowl. Then she took out a few different cheeses, cut them into small blocks and arranged them on a platter with some thin sliced cold cuts.

Instant charcuterie.

The spread was sad compared to what she would normally present, but given her current state of being, she was pleased with the outcome. Wine and a few bits of chocolate that she placed around the living room would have to be enough, she decided. She looked at the wine; two bottles of red. She went back to the liquor cabinet for a third.

That would be for her, she knew.

Everything was ready, and that left her plenty of time to get herself together. Making her way to the master, she poured over the simple dress collection she had acquired since moving to Singing Falls.

Her wardrobe was far simpler than what she had possessed when she lived in New York. But unlike before, her clothes now matched how she felt. Breezy, colorful, lightweight sundresses. Jeans that didn't threaten to cut off the circulation to her thighs, and comfortable shoes sans heels made up the majority of her daily wear now. Even though she didn't feel very bright, she chose a vibrant blue dress that she would wear over black leggings. Silver dangling earrings and a sapphire necklace completed the outfit.

Yes. It would work. She summoned a smile and looked herself over in the mirror. This would fool all of them; except perhaps Elric. While she missed the rapport her magic had allowed them to share, she was also grateful that the wolf could not get into her mind. At least not until she had a chance to do some major housekeeping in there.

She was convinced that if she faked something long enough, it would become truth.

Before she could second-guess anything, the doorbell rang. Walking through the house, she could make out voices and knew that it was Fionna and Glen. They were always early because Fionna was terrified of ever showing up late to an event and making a bad impression on someone.

"Hello, ladies," Torie said with a smile as she swung open the door.

"Hello yourself," said Fionna. She held up a bottle of wine, offering it to Torie.

"Fionna, I told you not to worry about bringing anything."

"We aren't up north," said Fionna. "No way we're showing up empty-handed."

Torie took the wine and stepped aside, letting her guests file in. Glen gave her a quick peck on the cheek and a squeeze on her upper arm as she passed.

"So, are you okay?" asked Fionna, spinning to face her friend.

"Yeah, I am. It's a beautiful day out. I'm glad the weather is finally turning."

"Oh not that," said Fionna. "I mean how are you doing with the loss of your magic?" Glen gave her a light elbow and a knowing look. "What? We're here to support her. But no one cares about the weather."

Torie chuckled good-heartedly. "Well, I care about the weather. But as for the other thing…I'm doing okay. I'm adjusting."

"I'm sorry," said Glen. "We certainly don't need to talk about this." She gave her wife another side eye glance.

"It's okay," said Torie. "I'm just trying to decide what to call myself. I'm not a witch anymore; but not sure I feel like a normal human either." She shrugged as she ushered them into the kitchen. "I didn't have a lot of time today to get much together, but please help yourself."

She took the bottle of wine Fionna had given her and added it to the collection on the island.

"There's already a bottle open, so feel free to help yourself," she said.

"Where's Jasmin?" asked Fionna. "I was sure she'd be here already."

"She texted. She's on her way."

"Any word from her sister?" Fionna asked.

Torie shook her head. She didn't want to think about the possibility that Jasmin's sister could help her regain her powers. The chance of failure would be too devastating.

"So are the guys coming over tonight?" Fionna asked.

"Not tonight," said Torie. "I thought it might be good to just have a girls' night for once." She noticed the look Glen gave her but refused to meet her eyes.

"Fine by me," added Fionna. "One on one they are fine. But the two of them together have a lot of testosterone."

Glen laughed. "That's because you haven't spent a lot

of time around men. It's just how they interact when they are together."

Fionna frowned. "Whatever. But honestly, the whole who is the- more- butch gets old fast."

Glen walked over to the island and started munching on some cheese. "So, have you seen much of Elric lately?" she asked, not looking up.

Torie started to answer, but a knock at the door interrupted her.

"And that would be Jasmin," she said, thankful for the distraction.

She opened the door, happy to see her friend and mentor. Just like Fionna, Jasmin came bearing a casserole dish and a paper bag.

"I brought some chicken buffalo dip and toasted pita chips," she said, leaning in to kiss Torie on the cheek. "I made it extra fattening…cos why the hell not."

"You didn't have to," said Torie, even though the smell of the dish made her stomach rumble.

"Oh I know. I wanted to." She breezed in, blowing past Torie with a smile. Walking into the kitchen, she exchanged greetings with Glen and Fionna and plopped her dish onto the island. "Oh good, plenty of wine. You know us so well."

"I have an idea," said Torie. "Why don't we sit out on the patio? It's a gorgeous day, and I could do with a little air."

They gathered the platters and headed out to the patio that overlooked a serene backyard that led to a line of old growth trees. Fionna made a second trip inside to get the glasses and wine before everyone settled on the teak furniture admiring the beauty of the fall colors that were just beginning to settle over the forestry.

"I love it back here," said Torie. Her voice was low and

her eyes took in the scenery without seeming to focus on any one aspect.

"How does it feel?" asked Jasmin.

Torie knew what she meant. Being able to sense her surroundings on a deeper level than just her normal five senses was something she had not even realized she possessed until it was gone.

"It's different. I'm not going to lie. Actually, it's almost scary at night."

"How's so?" asked Fionna.

"I can't explain it. I come out here and I feel like there are eyes on me. I never felt like that before."

"You're going to have to readjust to how you perceive nature," said Jasmin. "Your human senses are very different from the way your magic let you experience the world around you."

"Well, maybe she doesn't have to get accustomed to that,' added Fionna. "Has your sister gotten back to you yet?"

Jasmin didn't say anything, just looked sadly at the glass of wine she held.

"I'm sorry, Torie. Nothing yet. But she's always been a little flaky. Dropping out of touch and then springing back up unexpectedly. She'll get back to me. I'm sure of it."

Torie offered a smile. "It's really okay, Jasmin. I mean, I knew what I was doing. I still say it was worth it."

Even Fionna didn't argue that point. Torie's selfless act had probably saved them all.

"You know, even if my sister doesn't get back to me, I haven't given up. I'm still researching everything I can find about restoring a witch's powers. Plus, I'm calling in some favors with other witches in the area. Together, we'll find something."

Torie smiled and reached out, giving her friend's arm a light squeeze. "Thank you, Jasmin, I know you're doing everything you can. So no more talk about lost magic, okay?" said Torie. "I want to know what's going on with you guys?" She arched an eyebrow at them when no one spoke. "Well don't everyone talk at once."

"Well, we have news," said Glen, glancing over at Fionna. "I'm taking a new job."

"Oh yeah, doing what?" asked Jasmin.

"I'm starting a private first-responder business. One that focuses on the supernatural community. I spent so much time patching you guys up that I realized there was a market for it in town. I've been working with Max to potentially team up with the police division to deal with calls that most humans wouldn't understand."

"Wow," said Torie. "That's a great idea."

"Well, I figured that as long as you three are together, I probably won't have any shortage of business. Plus, at least this way I'll feel like I'm more of a help to you. Not just another non-supernatural who gets in the way."

She caught herself and gave a Torie a sharp, pained look.

"I am so sorry. I didn't mean that the way it sounded."

The fact that she made her friends uncomfortable made Torie feel awful.

"No, I didn't take it any way that wasn't intended. Besides, you have never not been helpful to us. I've always been thankful you were around with your trusty bag of medicines."

"It's been really well received," said Fionna. "We spent yesterday dropping her card off at some of the supernatural congregating spots around town. Just kind of getting the word out."

Just then, Glen's phone chirped, making everyone jump. She pulled it out of her pocket, frowning at the number that came up. Swiping at the screen, she held it to her ear.

"Hello?" She paused, nodding to herself. "I'll be right there." She slid it back into her pocket and looked at the others, excitement spreading over her face.

"Who was that?" asked Fionna.

"Talk about timing," Glen replied. "That was the owner of Jim's Bakery. He said a fight just broke out and there are a couple of supernaturals with injuries that need attention."

"A fight?" said Jasmin. "At...the coffee shop? This I gotta see."

Torie was on her feet and heading back into the house. She grabbed her keys from the console and headed for the door. "Well, what are we waiting for? I'll drive."

Chapter Two

They pulled up to the bakery in Torie's old Subaru and saw about a half-dozen people milling about on the sidewalk outside the shop. Before they could get out of the car, Jim, the owner, was racing towards them.

"Thank goodness you're here," he said to Glen. "I didn't know who to call. I mean, I love Sheriff Max and all, but I don't want my patrons being carted off to jail, and I sure don't want any unnecessary eyes prying into my business."

"What happened?" asked Jasmin.

He motioned for them to follow him. "Come on in and see for yourself."

They made their way into the bakery that Torie had come to think of as her home away from home. She had spent many mornings there, sitting in the comfortable leather chairs opposite the large, stone fireplace chatting away with Fionna and Jasmin. But for the first time since she had moved to Singing Falls, she felt ill at ease walking into the space.

Something was clawing at the back of her mind; and it made her skin crawl.

The place was in shambles. Coffee tables were upended, chairs had been tossed haphazardly about. The display counter that contained assorted homemade sweets and breads had been shattered, and one of the girls that worked behind the counter was sitting on the floor, back propped against the wall with a towel stained with blood held against her head.

Glen moved over to her first, bending down next to her and starting her examination.

"Jim, what happened here?" asked Jasmin, trying to take in the scene.

"I have no idea. One minute everything was fine; typical crowd. The next, chairs are flying and people were at each other's throats."

Torie looked around, taking mental snapshots of the crowd milling outside the large picture window and the ones still inside the shop. From the looks of things, it had been a busy evening. Nothing unusual about that. Torie could see where many of the patrons had been enjoying a cup of coffee with the delicious pastries the bakery was known for.

"Do you know who started it?" queried Jasmin.

Jim shrugged. "It all happened so fast. But I will say that the first blows were thrown by Jake Pressin and Mikey Belvin."

Jasmin gave him a surprised look.

"Those two are pretty much just kids. Good ones too. I can't see them throwing punches at anyone."

"You would think," said Jim. "But I'm telling you what I saw. There was nothing sweet about them. They had this crazed look in their eyes. Like they were just focused on one thing; hurting the other."

Jasmin wandered over to where Torie was looking around.

"Maybe those two were fighting over a girl. One of them said something to the other that was unflattering and...bam. Fight."

Jasmin shook her head. "Not those two. Jake is a rabbit shifter and Mikey is an empath. It isn't in either of their natures to come to physical blows. It's just not who they are."

Torie looked around, surveying the damage.

"Hey, Jim," she called, "was it just the two of them that did all this?"

"No," he replied. "It was like a scene out of a television show; once they threw the first punches, everyone in the place jumped up and started fighting. It was crazy."

Torie moved to the side of the room opposite the large fireplace. There was a small table for two that had not been disturbed. The white tablecloth was unruffled. There were two small plates, each with a slice of half-eaten carrot cake, and two cups of what appeared to be cinnamon tea. Torie looked at the setting and then glanced at the chaos around it.

Why hadn't it been overtaken by the wave of violence that washed over everything else?

"Jim, who was sitting here?" she asked.

The owner looked at the table and shook his head. "Sorry, I don't remember."

Torie started to tell him that was okay, but her attention was quickly drawn to a couple who had been peering into the wrecked place through the doorway. One yelled at the other and asked him to step back. The second man apparently took great affront to being spoken to that way and yelled back in response.

"Hey now," said Jim, stepping between them. "What's going on here?"

"He said your oatmeal cookies taste like they have almonds in them, and I said they taste more like walnuts," yelled one of the men. "He obviously doesn't know what he's talking about."

"You're a fool," said the second man, his voice rising. "You obviously wouldn't know a walnut if it walked up and punched you."

The first man bristled. "Oh yeah? How's this walnut taste?" He reached past Jim to swing at the man, his fist just grazing the man's jaw.

A roar escaped the one who was hit, and before anyone could step in, he shifted into a large bear, tossing Jim aside like a rag doll. The second man huffed audibly in and out of his nose. His breath sounded like the bellows of a forge, feeding a fire with its mighty wind. He shifted into a large bull, wide and muscular, the span of his horns nearly touching both walls either side of him. Someone outside screamed as patrons ran for cover.

The two shifters stared at one another, eyes glowing with hatred.

"Okay, that's enough!" screamed Jasmin.

She stepped forward, her hands clasped in front of her. Then she quickly separated them, sending an explosive shockwave outward that knocked the two shifters away from one another.

Their massive bodies crashed into walls and stonework, shaking the shop. Each of them struggled to their feet but immediately shifted back to human form. They were groggy, unsteady on their feet, holding their heads in their hands.

"What...what happened?" asked one of the men, looking around.

"You just tried to gore your friend here," said Jasmin, pointing at the bear shifter who was still trying to make his way to his feet.

"What? No. I...I would never do that."

Jasmin and Torie exchanged looks. Something was definitely amiss here.

"See that little lady over there with the black medicine bag?" said Jasmin. "Why don't you both go over there and let her look at you. We'll talk about what just happened later."

Torie rushed over to Jim's side. Fionna was there, trying to help the man to his feet.

"Did you see that?" Jim said, wincing at the pain that was rifling through his body. "Just like before. I've seen those two in here together many times. They're friends. But I'd swear if it weren't for Jasmin, one of them would have killed the other."

"He's right," said Fionna. "I could feel their anger. It was white hot. And there was something else as well..." her voice trailed off as a frown creased her brow.

"Fi, can you give me a hand here?" called Glen from behind the counter. She was starting to treat more of the cafe patrons who appeared to have suffered minor cuts and bruises.

"Coming!" said Fionna, bouncing for the back of the room.

"Well?" said Torie, as Jasmin walked back to her. "What did you feel?"

Jasmin shook her head. "I didn't feel anything. Just two men about to come to blows over cookies. It makes no sense whatsoever."

"You've been around supernaturals a lot longer than me," said Torie. "Could this just be part of their normal behavior? Something you're just now witnessing?"

"I don't think so. I mean, they were genuinely confused as to what was going on when they shifted back to human form. Like they didn't remember what set them off."

Torie found herself cursing her lack of magic. Again.

Just then, the sound of heavy boots crunching broken glass beneath them interrupted their conversation. They turned just as Sheriff Max walked up to them.

"Jasmin, Torie," he said, nodding at them in greeting.

"I thought Jim wasn't calling you?" Torie said.

"He didn't. Someone called into 9-1-1 to say that some of the special townfolk were having a quarrel at the coffee shop. Thought I'd see what it was about."

He whistled as he looked around, taking in the scene.

"Care to let me in on what happened?" he asked.

"Would if I could, Sheriff," said Jasmin. "But, honestly, we have no idea. People just seemed to flip and go at each other for a minute. But things seemed to have calmed down now."

The big sheriff nodded and then cocked his head to the side and sniffed the air, closing his eyes.

"What is it?" asked Torie. "You pick something up?"

"Magic," he said. "Just a whiff...now it's gone." Wolves were notorious for their sense of smell.

"That would be me," said Jasmin. "I had to whip up a little force field to separate two of the combatants."

Max nodded. "That would explain it then."

Torie snapped her finger. "Max, I have an idea. Would you come with me?"

The wolf frowned. "What are you doing involved in this Torie? You don't have any powers anymore."

She started, annoyed at his bluntness. "I know that. But it doesn't mean I can't hang out with my friends while they do…witchy things. Anyway, just follow me."

She led him to the back wall where the one table that had not been disturbed sat.

"Can you tell who was sitting here?" she asked.

Max looked around, to make sure no one was looking, and then leaned down to sniff the table. His face shimmered, shifting slightly; just enough to let his snout lengthen and thicken as his jawline receded into more lupine features. He took a deep breath through his nostrils, moving his face from side to side across the tabletop. Then he stood up, his face back to its normal handsome features.

"One person, female, human. Sat right there," he pointed to the left side of the table.

"And the other person?" asked Torie.

He shook his head. "There wasn't anyone else."

Torie looked from one side of the table to the other, pointing at the two distinct sets of dishes.

"You can see that there are clearly two partially eaten pieces of cake sitting on two different plates. Two different cups of tea and two different sets of silverware. She wasn't alone."

"I can see that, but I'm telling you what my nose told me. There was only one person sitting here. This side—" he gestured to the right side of the table, "—was vacant. No smell or trace of anyone or anything."

"That doesn't seem right."

He shrugged. "All I know is that I trust my nose; even more so than my eyes. And my nose says there was no one here."

He excused himself and went back to speak with Jim, eager to take the owner's statement.

Torie frowned and stood with her arms crossed, surveying the table. Then, glancing around to see if anyone was watching, she closed her eyes and held one hand over the table. She stood like that for nearly a full minute before being interrupted by someone clearing their throat. She spun around to see Jasmin staring intently at her.

"Anything?" Jasmin asked.

Torie let out a deep breath. "No. Of course not. I don't know what I keep hoping for."

Jasmin smiled warmly. "Keep hope alive, my friend. I still have some ideas to help with this."

Torie returned her smile but said nothing. She wasn't quite ready to give up on thinking that maybe one day her magic would return, but she also wasn't in the mood to get her hopes up only to have them dashed.

"What did Max say? Does he know who was sitting here?"

Torie shook her head. "He said there was only one person sitting here, A human woman. But no one else."

"Huh," said Jasmin. "That's weird."

"So now what?" said Torie. "Seems like there isn't anything more to this than random violence."

"Violence is never random. There is always a reason. We just need to figure out what it was."

They made their way back to the front of the building and walked outside.

"I guess we could talk to the people still hanging around," said Torie. "See if they saw anything that could explain what happened."

Jasmin agreed, and soon they had spoken to almost everyone outside the cafe. When they finished, Fionna and Glen came out to join them.

"How is everyone?' asked Torie.

"Bruised," said Glen. "A few cuts here and there, but for the most part, it was all superficial."

"Do any of them remember what started the melee?" asked Jasmin.

"No one knows anything. The two that Jasmin separated didn't even remember shifting," she added.

"Well, I think we've done all we can here. Looks like we won't be having our usual coffee and scones here tomorrow," said Torie. "This place is a mess."

"I'll swing by your place in the morning," said Jasmin. "Like I said, there is something I want to try. You make the coffee; I'll bring the treats."

They headed out, past the thinning crowd that was quickly losing interest in the goings-on at one of the local supernatural gathering spots in town.

They didn't notice the tall, pretty woman with afro-puffs that had been watching them intently through rose-colored sunglasses. Once they were in their cars and had left the drive, the young woman slipped around the back of the building where a window provided an unobstructed view of Max speaking with the shop owner.

She smiled. This was going to be easier than expected.

Chapter Three

True to her word, Jasmin arrived bright and early at Torie's house carrying an aluminum-covered plate that smelled divine. Torie ushered her in, and they made their way to the spacious kitchen.

"French press," said Torie, waving to the coffee press filled with an aromatic brown concoction. "I picked up some organic Robusta and thought it deserved something other than a drip coffee maker."

"You will never hear me complain about French press coffee. I just hope this will live up to it."

She removed the foil to reveal a beautiful, rustic, French apple tart.

"I guess we both had the French on our minds today," she said. "Here, hand me a knife and I'll start cutting and plating this; you pour the coffee."

Torie did as she was asked, trying to ignore the rumble in her stomach. The combination of fresh pastry and coffee too much for her.

"This is nice," Torie said. "Honestly, I haven't had much

of an appetite lately. With everything going on, I just don't feel like eating."

"Or cleaning, it would seem," said Jasmin, making it a point to acknowledge the dirty dishes in the sink.

"I'll get to them…eventually."

Torie poured two coffees and sat the cups on a serving tray with a small sugar bowl and a tiny pitcher of cream.

"Why don't we eat out on the patio? The air is so nice and crisp. It will be nice."

Jasmin smiled. "Sure. I wait all year for the chance to wear these big bulky sweaters, so why not?"

They settled on one of the comfortable teak sofas, with an overflowing tray of autumn goodness in front of them. The leaves on the trees laid out before them were just beginning to change, taking on the vibrant red and oranges that would soon have the canopy looking like it was awash in flames. They didn't speak, each enjoying the silence of the other's company in the way only close friends could.

Finally, Jasmin cleared her throat. "Okay, so real talk. It's just me and you. How are you coping?"

Torie sat her cup down and stared into the distance, collecting her thoughts before she could answer. "Well, I'm trying not to get caught up in the drown-my-sorrows-in-a-bottle-of-wine trap each night if that's what you mean."

Jasmin smiled, her eyes filled with compassion.

"No, that isn't exactly what I meant. If you need to drink yourself under the table to get through this, then that's what you need to do. Just know that I'll be here to pick you up and clean you off if I have to. But I didn't mean what are your coping mechanisms…I meant how are *you*?"

"I know. It's just hard to talk about. I feel like I'm mourning someone that I never really knew. I have to keep reminding myself that I didn't have magic for over forty years of my life; I'll be fine for another forty without it." Saying the words out loud made them more real somehow. She felt hollow inside; but knew that acceptance was the first step in getting on with her life.

"Don't be so fatalistic," said Jasmin. "You've never seemed like the type to just give up. Look at everything you've been through; all that you've endured. You're stronger than this, Torie."

"I would like to think that is true. But I'm telling you, I don't feel it anymore. When my magic first manifested itself, I knew there was something different going on, deep inside me." She pressed her fist to her chest for emphasis. "But now, I don't feel that anymore. Not even a tingle of it inside me."

"Well, that's what I'm here for. I want to work with you to see what we can do. I need to see if there is any spark that I can still feel."

Torie looked at her expectantly. "Do you think your magic can bring mine back?"

Jasmin sipped her coffee. "I don't know, but we can try. You were able to force it out; maybe another witch can bring it back."

"Have you ever heard of this happening before?"

Jasmin looked away before answering. "No. I've never heard of a case of a witch losing her powers before. Hexes are primal magic; it belongs to the one who wields it for life. I even made some calls to other witches in the area. No one knew such a thing was even possible."

"Other witches? You mean here in Singing Falls?"

"A few yes. And ones in neighboring towns. We aren't the only ones, you know."

Torie nodded. "You mean like your sister?"

Jasmin gave her a side-eyed glance. "Yes. Like her."

Torie shifted her weight so she was fully facing her friend. "So why haven't you spoken about her? I asked Fionna and she said she knew you had a sister, but that was all. That in all the time the two of you have known each other, you haven't really spoken about her."

Jasmin looked uncomfortable. "We aren't here to talk about me. We're here to try and get you your magic back."

Normally, Torie was not the type to pry. Especially when it came to family matters. That was a giant can of worms she wasn't fond of venturing into with people. But Jasmin was different. She had felt a kinship with her from the moment they met. They had literally saved one another's lives on more than one occasion.

If you couldn't pry into someone like that, then who could you? Besides, she sensed that her friend wanted to talk about it.

"Yes, you're right," said Torie, "we are trying to get my powers back. And if you have faith in someone to help do that, then I'd like to have faith in them as well. But that means I need to know a little more about them."

Jasmin took a deep breath and let it out slowly.

"I guess I can't really argue with that. But yes, I do have faith my sister could help you. Like I said, she is a witch doctor, and a powerful one at that."

Torie interrupted. "Alright, before you go any further, explain to me what exactly a witch doctor is?"

"Basically, she is a witch whose power is focused on the spirit world. That gives her a great insight into what ails people. Especially someone magical. She can not only see their auras, but she can delve into their very spirit and interact with it."

"So you think she can help me?"

"I hope so."

"Hope isn't a strategy," answered Torie.

"No, but it might be all we have right now, so hold onto it."

Both women were silent for a moment, each sipping tea and eating forkfuls of pastry.

"This is amazing," said Torie between mouthfuls. "I didn't know you could cook like this."

"Oh, I can't cook. But I can bake like nobody's business." She winked at Torie and raised her cup of coffee in salutations.

"So. It sounds like you have a lot of pride in your sister and her skills," said Torie.

"Yes, I guess I do."

"So why haven't you ever talked about her before? What happened between the two of you? And don't tell me it's nothing. I don't have a sibling, but if I did, I'd like to think we would keep in contact. When was the last time you spoke with her?"

Jasmin narrowed her eyes. "Didn't you tell me you and your mother went years without speaking?"

Torie felt herself blush. "Yes. And I also told you that I regretted every minute of that. There are some things that you can't have a re-do for."

Again, Jasmin sighed. "Well, it's been a few decades since we talked."

Torie snorted, nearly choking on her coffee. "Decades? Are you telling me it's been over twenty years?"

Jasmin nodded, unable to meet her friend's gaze.

"How do you know she's even still alive?" Torie almost wished she could swallow the words back as soon as she voiced them.

Jasmin read her discomfort and smiled. "It's okay. She's

23

alive. We may not have contact, but believe me, I'd know if something happened to her. It's stretched thin, but we're still connected." She shrugged. "It's a witch thing I guess."

Torie didn't know what to say at that point, so she said the only thing that popped into her mind. "I always wanted a sister. Someone I could share secrets with. Someone to swap clothes with. Someone who would have my back growing up when my mom was being unrealistic. Someone I could trust with everything, and vice versa."

Jasmin nodded. "We were like that growing up. We were inseparable. She is older than me by a couple of years and our grandmother couldn't wait for our powers to develop... to see what we would become."

"Wait, your grandmother told you she was a witch?"

"Absolutely. She would show us all the incredible things she could do and tell us that one day, we would be able to do them as well. She began prepping us for our powers early on. Our mother wasn't too thrilled but that was because she was just coming into her own powers and was scared of them."

Torie frowned. "But if you haven't spoken with your sister in so long, how do you know what her powers were? Didn't they develop after you turned forty? And that would mean you stopped communication before that happened, right?"

"Yes, you are right. But we were tested early to see what kind of hex witches we would be. Being from a line of paranormal beings that most people in the south were afraid of, Grams left nothing to chance. She told our mother we needed to know what our powers would be so we could prepare for our future. One day, a traveling carnival came to town—you know, the kind that put up Ferris wheels and other death-traps overnight. Well, this particular carnival had a fortune teller, so our mother decided that it was time we had our fortunes told."

"Wait, hold up a minute. You mean fortune tellers are real?"

"Most of them? Not at all. But every now and then you'll stumble across the real thing. My mother's magic told her this one was the real deal. As soon as we walked in, the teller recognized our lineage and immediately dispensed with all the hokum that she usually used to con those who wanted to believe out of extra money.

"She took one look at us and said I would follow in my mother's footsteps with magic that was hard to master at first and was best handled by an aggressive personality. With my sister, she said that she would walk in both worlds...that of the living and that of the spirits. She said she would be very powerful and the spirits would smile on her; granting her the power of vision and mastery over wayward spirits. We were twelve at the time."

"And like me, you both got your powers after turning forty?"

"Mine came the day of my fortieth birthday. I have a feeling Opal's did as well."

"When was the last time you saw one another?"

"At our mother's funeral." She choked up, the words refusing to continue.

Torie reached over and placed a hand on her friend's arm. "It's okay. We don't have to talk about this."

Jasmin shook her head, motioning that she was okay. She took a sip of coffee and then continued.

"She was killed...she gave her life protecting me and Opal from a Tommyknocker. Do you know what that is?"

Torie shook her head, eyes wide as Jasmin continued.

"A Tommyknocker is a very particular type of ghost. It's

the ghost of a man killed in a mining accident. When we were fifteen, our father was killed in a mine. That was the only job an uneducated man in the south could get at that time. He worked ridiculous hours for barely enough to keep us fed and a roof over our head."

Her eyes began to mist up, filling with emotions long held back.

"Anyway, one day there was a knock on the door. It was the town sheriff, delivering the news that every coal miner's wife dreaded. There was a collapse at the mine...no idea how bad it was. Opal and I joined our mom at the site along with all the other wives, waiting into the night and then the next day for word.

"When word came, we were told that everyone in the mine had perished. And to make matters worse, the collapse was so bad it meant the bodies couldn't be recovered. When the shock settled, the mine paid out claims to all the families. It was enough, barely, for one of us to go to college. Opal, having always been the, how shall I put this...less structured of us, decided I should be the one to go to college. She had other plans she said, though she would never tell me what they were.

"But then, one night when our mother was out, I caught her in the woods behind our house. She was trying to perform a magic ritual, even though she had no powers at the time. She had an old book of incantations from some back-alley bookstore in town. That, combined with some foul smelling candles and a Ouija board was all she thought she needed to speak with our father. She was convinced that if she would one day have the power to command the spirits, she would jumpstart her magic by compelling our father to come back to us."

Torie sat silently, one hand over her mouth. She barely breathed, her attention focused on Jasmin.

"I begged her not to, but she was intent on doing it. She said that there was no way our dad's life should have been cut so short. It couldn't have been his time to go, so that meant she should be able to get him back. She begged me to help her, to combine our non-existent power and demand that the Ouija board return him to us. She read some phrases aloud from the book…I have no idea what they were, they sounded Latin; then we lit some candles and turned to the board.

"We had no idea what we were doing, or the ramifications of our ignorance. We called to our father, asked any spirits that were listening to bring him back. And then, in her arrogance, Opal commanded them to obey her. She demanded that our father return to us.

"When nothing happened, we finally gave up and went back home. That very night, while we were sleeping, it came. A spirit that had been twisted by the darkness that lives in mines."

"What kind of darkness?" Torie asked.

"I don't know for sure, but in my time, I've found anyplace that is a source of misery to those who spent time there, takes on those negative, black emotions; and can then pass those feelings on to the spirits of the ones who die there. That's why you see so many hauntings in old hospitals, prisons, plantations, and mines. Places whose residents carry so much sadness in them that it becomes a part of their surroundings.

"That was what came to visit us that night. A black spirit, darker than the night around it, fueled by sadness and hate and called forth in the name of our father. It attacked us, in ways that I still have nightmares about. It couldn't be reasoned with or controlled. It lashed out, tearing at us. It would have killed us, but our mother heard the commotion in the room we shared and came to help us. For some reason, the spirit became fixated on her…ripping into her, crushing her.

"Opal and I ran from the house, ran as fast as we could to our Gram's house. We told her what had happened, and she told us to stay in her house, and not to step outside the threshold, no matter what, until morning. She left us there, huddled in her one-bedroom house that was little more than a shack, while she made her way to our house.

"The next morning, she came back. We knew immediately that something terrible had happened. She didn't speak for a while. When she finally did, she said that she had been too late for our mother. And that it had taken everything she had to repel the spirit and send it back to whatever hell it had come from. She looked at us differently from that day…I'm sure she knew what we had done, but she never asked.

"The funeral for our mother was the last time I saw my sister. There were a lot of hurt feelings and misplaced blame between us. Our Gram passed shortly thereafter. She was just never the same after that night. I guess seeing her own daughter like that sapped whatever light she had left in her.

"So as a result, I was alone when I came into my magic. I learned what I could from who I could." She looked at Torie and gave her a warm smile. "I guess that's why I'm so intent on helping you. No one should have to weather what we go through alone."

The two friends looked at one another, both feeling raw and exhausted from such a deep, emotional dive. Then Jasmin reached up with both hands and lightly wiped the tears from her face.

"Girl, enough about all that sadness. We need to get you back in the magic game." She stood up and offered a hand to help Torie to her feet. "And I have just the thing that might help."

She gestured, and the large purse she carried everywhere floated to her hand. She reached in and withdrew a vial of liquid and a handful of glowing stones of various colors.

"These are enchanted gems that were given to me by a rock troll."

"And what exactly do they do?"

"Well, I'm hoping they will help you get some aspect of your magic back while we wait for my sister. If you're brave enough for a little experiment."

She looked at Torie and offered a wink. Together, they went back into the house. Torie's heart hammered in her chest as she tried to keep hope alive, but not let that hope swell too much inside her soul.

Chapter Four

"So how do these troll rocks work?" asked Torie.

They were sitting in the living room with the colored gems spread on the coffee table before them.

"First, they're not rocks, they are gems. Big difference." Jasmin leaned forward, taking one of the red stones in her hand and holding it up for Torie to see. "Second, they are suffused with earth magic. Meaning they are connected to the same wellspring our own magic flows from; good old Mother Earth."

She opened her hand so the gem lay flat on her palm.

"Ignitus," she whispered. The gem flared to life, releasing red and orange flames that flickered. "In the case of the gems, the magic comes from inside them, not from inside us."

"Okay, so how does that help me get my magic back?"

"Well, and this is just a theory, but maybe your magic isn't gone. Maybe it's blocked. If you can work with these gems, maybe we can get you unclogged. Consider these training wheels to getting you back on the bike. Here——" she stopped the fire and handed the gem to Torie, "——you try."

Torie took the stone in her hand. Amazingly, it was actually cold to the touch, despite having been fully engulfed in fire just seconds before.

She held it flat on her palm and whispered the same incantation. One she had used countless times over the past months.

Nothing. No flame. Not even a spark.

She looked at Jasmin questioningly.

"Are you concentrating? You can't just be going through the motions."

Torie furrowed her brow, focusing her intent on making the little gem flare to life. In her mind she pictured the fire and fixed that image in place, willing the gem to ignite.

"Ignitus," she said forcefully. Again, nothing happened.

"Hmm. Let me try something." Jasmin leaned forward and whispered to the gem. Instantly it burned bright with mystical fire.

"Ouch!" shouted Torie, tossing the gem to the ground and grasping her singed hand.

Instantly, Jasmin doused the flame and looked at her friend's reddened palm.

"That shouldn't have happened. The power in the gems is part of our magical eco-systems. It shouldn't hurt us."

Torie nodded, staring at her hand. "So what does that mean?" Even though she had a good idea what it meant.

"I'm not sure. Maybe your blockage runs deeper than I thought."

Torie stood, walking to the corner of the room where there was a large aloe plant growing. She broke a tip off one of the small leaves and rubbed the viscous liquid that oozed out onto her hand. The cooling liquid took away the sting almost immediately.

"Or maybe, we just need to face the facts," she said as she made her way back to the couch.

"You know, you need to get your magic back for all kinds of reasons," Jasmin said. "First and foremost, I need my friend back at full hex so we can continue the work we started here in the community."

"Oh, so you do enjoy helping people," Torie said, breaking into a smile.

"I mean…maybe it's been more fulfilling, and fun, than I thought. Minus the close calls with death; that I can do without. But yes, we are filling a much needed niche in our society. But also, you have made a name for yourself in the supernatural world. We all have. I don't like the thought of you being unable to protect yourself if the need arises."

This was something Torie had not considered. "You think I might be in danger at some point?"

"Honestly, I don't know. But you've been responsible for taking out a serial killer, a vampire and a warlock. All I'm saying is, this town is not as sleepy as it once was. More and more paranormals are moving in almost daily. All of them can't be friendlies."

"Well, there are also plenty of humans living in Singing Falls now. They don't seem to be afraid."

"True, but they do seem a little more nervous than usual. Granted, they don't know all the supernaturals in the community, but they know that this town is anything but normal. That little scrap at Jim's Bakery didn't help calm the masses."

"True. We still don't know what happened to cause that. Something about it just didn't feel…right."

"And that's another reason we need to get your powers

back. You can't go into hot zones like that again with no magic." She reached out, picking up another gem. This one was the color of a sapphire, with rough cut edges and only slightly larger than the red stone from earlier. "The red gems generate heat and fire. The blue ones generate pure light. The white ones emit energy blasts, and the green ones are for communication over distance. Kind of like magical walkie talkies. These are all gems meant to replicate some of the magic your hexes granted you."

"Wait, I didn't know that witches could communicate over distance with one another."

"Sure you did. Think of it as telepathy. Though in your case, it worked better with shifters. It was that hex ability that allowed you to communicate with them."

Torie felt a lump form in her throat as she stared at the green gem on her table. The connection she felt with the shifter community, and Elric in particular, was what she missed the most. Maybe it was because that was the first of her abilities to develop and the one she had felt most at ease with.

"So, what's going on with Elric?" Jasmin asked.

Torie squinted at her. "No peeking inside my mind."

Jasmin held up both hands. "Hey, I would never. But I guess that means you are thinking about him." She smiled and gave her friend's knee a squeeze. "No one needs to be a mind reader to know that something is going on with the two of you."

Torie nodded reluctantly. "I don't know what it is. I get the feeling that, ever since I lost my magic, he's been treating me like a fragile child. That I need to be placed in a plastic bubble at all times and kept away from furniture with sharp edges." She slumped back into the couch with a sigh. "I mean, I'm not that delicate. I managed to keep myself alive for a long time without even knowing that magic existed. I still remember how to…how to human!"

Jasmin didn't say anything, just letting her friend contemplate what she had said.

"Are you sure it's him who is feeling that way, or are you projecting that onto him? You know, werewolves are not the bloodthirsty, alpha male, top dog that a lot of people think they are. I don't mean this to sound rude, but think of them like big, cuddly…well, dogs. They are very familial creatures. They form bonds to their pack that are, for the most part, unbreakable.

"And they mate for life. If he has chosen you…he will move Heaven and earth to protect you. He will be loyal to you no matter what happens, and he will never be happier than when he is looking into your eyes. You're a very lucky woman.

"So no matter what you're feeling right now…my guess is, he's giving you time to work through it, no matter how long it takes. And he'll be there when you come out the other side."

Torie thought about this as she remained quiet, deep in contemplation.

"The truth is, I'm glad he's around. I have always felt safe with him, and I hope he knows that. I just need a bit of time to adjust to what's happening to me."

"Hey, I'm not the one you need to be telling that to."

"You're right. You're absolutely right. I'll talk to him. But in the meantime, what do we do with all these gems? It's not like I need them now. I'm not even sure why you brought them, knowing my magic is gone."

"Not gone, blocked," replied Jasmin, projecting confidence. "And I want them here, because like I said, it's practice for you. Think of them as you would a thigh-blaster.

When you're not doing anything just give them a little squeeze...start to build those muscles back up." She stood up, heading for the fireplace and taking the red one with her. "Maybe we'll just leave this one in here...no need to risk third degree burns." She tossed the gem into the wood piled in the fireplace, and then turned to face Torie.

"I want to do something else for you as well," she said. "I want to place some wards around your house. Nothing big, just something to act as a first line of defence against anyone who means you harm."

Torie wasn't sure how she felt about that, and Jasmin could tell from the look on her face she wasn't sure it was needed.

"Think of it as a supernatural alarm system; always set and ready in case you need it. And if you don't need it, no harm, no foul."

Finally, Torie agreed. "Alright, if you think it's needed. But what if it goes off? What do I do?"

"Well, if something sets it off, you won't have to do anything but stay inside the house. I'll know if it happens and I'll be here before you know it."

Again, Torie felt like a burden to her friends. That plastic bubble she imagined Elric wanted to lock her in was starting to feel more and more real. She nodded, knowing that eventually Jasmin would wear her down anyway.

She watched her friend as she moved to the center of the living room and brought her hands together before her, eyes closed. To Torie it looked like she was praying, except that the prayer was accompanied by intricate finger inter-locking and hand motions as Jasmin weaved her spell.

"There," Jasmin said, looking up. "I have invoked the guardians of the four corners to protect your home. It should be proof against whatever might come prowling around looking to start trouble. Now, one last thing." She walked over to the coffee table and picked up the white gem. "I want you to keep this one on you at all times."

"Thanks, Jasmin, but I can't make it work. It won't respond to my magic."

"That's okay. I already enchanted it. It will work almost the way the wards around your house do. If you're in trouble or distressed, it will fire a bolt of force magic. Think of it as a mystical snub-nosed .38 special."

Torie eyed the gem suspiciously. "I don't like guns, and I don't know if I should be impressed or scared that you know so much about them."

"Hey, growing up, guns weren't just for protection. There were plenty of times we wouldn't have eaten if it weren't for my dad's rifle."

Torie didn't speak, just regarded her friend with admiration. Her own upbringing had not been so severe. Her mother had always provided a nice life for her. Not the type she had come to know with her ex-husband of course, but certainly a far cry from what Jasmin had experienced. Thinking of her mother shot a dagger of pain through her heart. She glanced at the green gem as thoughts flashed through her mind. Maybe...

"So," said Jasmin. "Are you going to keep the white gem with you? At all times?"

Torie snapped out of her reverie. "Yes. And thank you. For everything you're doing."

She meant that. She had never known friends like the kind she had made here in Singing Falls. She truly believed they would do anything for her; and with or without magic, she knew she would do anything for them as well.

"Okay then," said Jasmin. "Good to know. Now, it's

afternoon, so what say we break out some cocktails? A girl gets thirsty with all the soul-sharing and whatnot."

Torie laughed and headed for the kitchen, making her way to the wood and glass liquor cabinet that sat in the far corner of the space.

Just then, Jasmin's phone beeped twice, letting her know someone was texting her. She looked down at it, stopping in her tracks.

"What is it?" asked Torie.

"It's from Max. He said there's a vicious fight that's broken out at Nightshades."

Torie felt her heart catch in her throat. "Why do I know that name?"

"It's the bar where humans and supernaturals go to commingle. It's where Wednesday went to meet the warlock. He's saying it's bad."

Together, they raced out the door. Torie paused long enough to grab the white troll gem and shove it in her pocket. She wasn't sure it would matter to her, but if she was walking into anything like what happened at the bakery, a gun was better than nothing at all.

Chapter Five

Nightshades was a rambling, one-story bar-slash-restaurant that squatted at the end of a gravel drive on the outskirts of town. It had a reputation as being a hard hitting, hard drinking dive where supernaturals could congregate with the humans that were brave enough to set foot inside. As the younger kids would say, it was a hook-up bar; one where humans who wanted to get to know the darker side of Singing Falls could go. While it may have been imposing, it was also known to be a fairly quiet spot.

The supernaturals that frequented it felt comfortable because they could be themselves, and the humans that went there never started anything because they understood that in this place, they were on the lowest rung of the food chain. That made the bar Switzerland in the eyes of Singing Falls. It operated under a very simple motto that was written in bold red lettering on a pine board hanging behind the counter: Don't Start Nothing, Won't Be Nothing.

When Torie and Jasmin arrived, the scene looked much the same as that at the bakery. Tables had been overturned, bar stools were thrown about, the large mirror behind the bar had been shattered, and there were a considerable number of broken dishes and silverware scattered about the main floor of the space.

There were quite a few shifters and humans alike sitting in various booths around the periphery of the dining area. Some held their heads in their hands, some were lying back in the booths, recovering.

"What the hell happened?" Jasmin said, walking up to Max.

The werewolf stood surveying the damage all around him. A stern look passed over his features as he motioned for her and Torie to follow him to the side of the bar, away from everyone else.

"Was it the same as what happened at the bakery? Just random violence breaking out?" asked Torie.

"Not sure. From what I understand, it was just a normal day here, then an argument broke out between a couple of regulars; then this," he said.

Torie looked around. The bar had been crowded. "It's barely after midday. Are people really here drinking at this time?"

Max shrugged. "This place is jumping at all hours. It's known for weekend brunches believe it or not. Trouble here is rare. And it certainly doesn't happen in the middle of the day like this."

"I've actually been here for brunch before," said Jasmin. "This was one of Taylor's favorite spots. She'd drag me and Fionna here every couple of months. Max is right…no one causes trouble here."

"What about the staff and owner? Did they say what caused the argument?" asked Torie.

"Apparently it was a fox shifter and a wood elf that got

into it. They were seen whispering together at the bar, then their voices started to rise and before you knew it, one hit the other over the head with a beer glass. Then they started tussling...which caused them to knock the beer over on a man sitting next to them. He flew into a rage and just started swinging at everyone. Before he knew it, the whole place was brawling."

"Everyone?" said Jasmin.

"What do you mean?" replied Max.

"Well, a lot of the furniture that is destroyed are big, heavy pieces. That bench—" she pointed to the wall, "—was ripped loose from the floor where it was bolted down. The jukebox over there used to be against the wall opposite it. That means it was thrown. This was a fight among supernaturals...and it doesn't look like they were holding back."

"Okay. And?" he responded.

"Where are the humans?" said Torie, looking around. "Everyone touts this as a meeting place between humans and supernaturals. If an all-out fight broke out, I don't think the humans would have survived any of this."

"They wouldn't have," said Jasmin. "They ran. I'm betting there were no reports of human injuries, huh?" She turned to Max for confirmation.

Jasmin joined her as they walked around the bar.

"Where were the two who started this sitting?" asked Torie.

"Hold on," replied Max as he went over to the bar. "Hey, Mica, can you come over for a second?"

They were joined by a young bartender dressed in denim and a tight white sleeveless tee shirt.

"Can you help us out here? The two that started the fight, where were they seated?"

"This way," she said, escorting them to the very end of the bar. "They were the last two at the end, here."

"And you've seen them in here before?" asked Max.

She nodded. "Yes, typically they are here almost every Friday night, but they sometimes come in during the day as well."

"And they've always tolerated one another?" questioned Jasmin.

"Oh yeah, they're friends. At least they were."

Torie walked from the end of the bar to the booth that was closest to it. There, on the table in the booth was a plate with a half-eaten quarter chicken on it, sitting across from a bowl of what looked to be tomato bisque. Two glasses of iced tea sat next to the food, undisturbed.

"What is it?" asked Jasmin.

Torie pointed at the meal. "Just like at the bakery. These are just about the only meals that aren't smashed in the whole bar." She turned to the young bartender. "Who was sitting here?"

The bartender shrugged. "I don't know. A woman and some guy I believe."

Torie looked at Max and nodded. He bent over the booth and sniffed the air.

"Yes, same woman as the one at the bakery. Also, same 'nothing' here where her companion sat," he said.

"Jasmin, this can't be a coincidence," Torie muttered. She turned back towards Mica. "Can you describe them?"

"Not really. I mean, they just looked like a couple of humans sitting there. They weren't drinking so I didn't pay them much attention." She turned to go back to cleaning up the mess of broken bottles behind the counter but stopped, turning to face them. "Jimmy might be able to tell you more. He was the server that brought them the meal. He seemed pretty friendly with them…like he knew them."

"Who's Jimmy?" said Torie.

"He's a kid who does dishes and helps bus tables. But he got swept up in the fighting. He's pretty banged up. He's out back being tended to by that nurse who showed up to patch everyone up."

"Glen? She and Fionna must be here," said Jasmin.

"Thank you, Mica," said Max. "You've got a nasty cut on your arm there. Better go get it checked."

She laughed and smiled coyly at the werewolf. "Thanks. But I'll heal. Maybe it will leave a cute scar I can show you sometime." She turned on her heels and headed back to her work.

"Haven't you learned your lesson with those lynx shifters?"

They turned to see Elric walk into the bar. His eyes landed on Torie and he nodded to her, smiling.

"Their meow isn't as bad as their scratch," said Max, shaking hands with his old friend.

"Elric," said Torie, moving to stand next to him. "How did you know what was going on here?"

"Everyone in town knows. Well, that and I asked Max here to keep me in the loop whenever something like this happened."

Torie shot the sheriff a look, one that he didn't meet. Whatever his reasoning for keeping Elric appraised, she was thankful.

"I mean, if you'd rather I not be here…" Elric started.

"Don't be ridiculous," said Torie. "It's a free town after all."

Why did she say that? She silently cursed herself. She

was acting like a schoolgirl who was feeling ignored by the football captain she had a crush on.

"Finally. The gang's all here," came a voice from one of the booths on the opposite side of the bar.

Everyone looked over as a figure stood up out of the bar and turned to face them. It was a woman, probably in her early twenties, tall and lithe of build. She moved like a dancer as she approached them. She wore leather pants and a matching leather jacket. Her dark skin was highlighted by the white tee shirt that left her abdomen exposed. She had a cigarette in one hand which she casually flicked to the side.

"Who are you?" demanded Torie.

"Not important," she responded. "But I was starting to think he wasn't going to show up." She nodded in Elric's direction.

"Do you know him?" said Torie.

"No. But I need both of them. So, if you two ladies could move to the side, I have work to do." One hand snaked to her waist where she withdrew a foot-long dagger from a sheathe strapped to her thigh. "You there; Max. I almost took you out at that weird little coffee shop everyone seems to love. But then I thought if I killed you, the other one might go on the run." She looked from Max to Elric, her hazel eyes sharp and focused. "And I need both your pelts for the payday."

Elric and Max looked at one another.

"A hunter," Max said, turning his attention back to the girl. "Get them out of here, Elric."

He moved faster than the witches could follow, sprinting towards the young woman, shifting into his wolf form just as he reached her. He leapt upward, meaning to take her down and pin her beneath his considerable weight. But his attack had been anticipated, and the young woman reached out, her speed matching his, as she grabbed a handful of his hide. Pivoting on her hind foot, she threw the wolf behind her, sending his body crashing through two booths and into a wall with a sickening crunch.

"Hey!" came a voice from behind the bar.

Mica leapt over the counter and charged the woman. She growled as she approached, reaching for the hunter with blinding speed.

The hunter caught her wrist mid-strike, holding the lynx shifter aloft with one hand.

"Really?" said the hunter. "Are you really trying to stop me?" She shot her free hand forward, punching Mica in the chest and sending her body rocketing across the bar.

A growl, followed by a deep roar, shook the building. Max had regained his feet and was circling the hunter. The hair along the ridge of his back stood stiff and his fangs glistened as he took the full measure of the woman.

"Torie, Jasmin, you have to get out of here. Now," said Elric. He began to shift into his hybrid form, his limbs elongating as his face twisted into a combination of human and wolf. He stood there, eight feet of fangs and claws, his eyes glued to his once alpha as he slowly marched around the hunter. He turned to face Torie, his yellow eyes pleading.

"I can't hear what you're saying, Elric," she said. "But if you're telling us to run, the answer is no."

"Actually it's 'hell no'," said Jasmin. She held up her hands, summoning magic in the form of glowing blue orbs that encircled her fists. She turned to face the hunter and took a step forward.

Elric placed a large paw gently on her chest, looking from her to Torie.

Jasmin understood and backed up to stand next to her friend. Elric roared, and then turned, charging the hunter.

The building shook beneath the weight of his footsteps as he advanced. He glanced at Max, nodding at some unspoken communication that passed between them.

As one, they attacked the hunter, lunging and slashing at the woman.

The blade was the object of their first attack. Max feinted one direction and then spun with blinding speed as he attacked her from the left. She pivoted, using her free hand to shield her side. At the same instant, Elric made a grab for her right arm, trying to pry the blade free. His attack worked as the knife flew from her hand to skitter across the wooden floor.

The hunter grunted, lifting her knee to connect with Elric's jaw before he could sink his fangs into her. Simultaneously, she twisted her body, driving her elbow downward on to Max's spine. The wolf howled in pain as the blow drove him into the ground.

She spun then, lashing out with a kick that connected with his jaw, slamming it shut. She reached down, wrapping her arm around his neck. She meant to snap the werewolf's spine, but before she could gain sufficient leverage, Elric was at her back again. This time, he grabbed her about the waist in a bear hug, lifting her off his friend.

The hunter grunted as he sought to squeeze the wind from her lungs. She drove an elbow backward into his mid-section and followed that up by slamming the back of her head into his snout. Elric howled in pain, relaxing his grip on her just enough for the hunter to slip her arms free of his hold. She reached up, grasped him about the head, and pulled his body up and over her own, slamming him to the floor with a thud.

She rolled across the floor, sweeping up her knife in a single, graceful move. Then, knife in hand, cartwheeled backwards to straddle Elric's still stunned body. With one hand she held the werewolf in place, while lifting the knife over her head as she prepared to deliver the death blow. A flash of blue light struck her knife hand, sending it spiraling away from her.

The hunter looked over to see Jasmin send another blast of power her way. She rolled to the side, barely evading the bolt of light. One hand snaked inside her jacket, and as she came up out of the roll, she flicked a small, black blade at Jasmin. It whizzed past the witch's head, embedding itself in the wall behind her. At this point, she sensed Max approaching from behind, and she spun, catching him with a spinning heel kick that knocked the wolf sideways.

Reaching into another hidden pocket in her jacket, she withdrew a golden sphere that was connected to a gold chain that shimmered to life in her grasp. She begun to spin it rapidly before her just as Jasmin unleashed another bolt of magic. The power hit the whirling gold chain and splintered into sparks of harmless light. With the chain and sphere acting as a shield before her, she slowly advanced on the witch.

A blast of thunder rocked the bar as a section of the ceiling above the hunter exploded. At the same time, glowing ectoplasmic tentacles stretched up from the floor, wrapping themselves around the hunter and then tossing her hard against the back wall.

Everyone looked behind where the hunter had stood. Glen was there reloading her shotgun. At her side stood Fionna and another woman dressed in gray jeans, a red button-up shirt and a long, silver cardigan. Her eyes glowed white and her body seemed to glow with the same, eerie light that had emanated from the tentacles. The distinctive *chc-chock* sound of the shot gun as Glen pumped the shells into place froze everyone.

"Let's see if you can block this," Glen said, her voice flat as she aimed the barrel at the young woman.

The hunter slowly looked around her, realizing she was surrounded. Jasmin stood before her, both fists glowing with magic, the two wolves had regained their feet and were stalking her from both sides. Behind stood Glen with a loaded shotgun and the woman who had summoned yet more ghostly tentacles that floated next to her.

The hunter smiled and slowly raised both hands to the ceiling.

Max shifted back to human form and carefully approached her.

"Elric, get my cuffs from my jacket over on the bar. Don't you move, little lady." He slowly grasped one of her wrists and brought her arm back behind her.

The hunter moved with blinding speed. She twisted her body, crossing her wrists to break the surprised werewolf's grip. Then, scooping him up like a rag doll, she tossed him at both Glen and the stranger, sending the three of them crashing over the bar. An errant shotgun blast went off in Elric's direction, causing him to dive for cover.

The hunter seized on the distraction to disappear, somersaulting out the door and running away from the bar into the woods.

Chapter Six

"Elric, let's go!" shouted Max. The two wolves were out the door and sprinting towards the woods before anyone could stop them.

"Opal?" said Jasmin as she approached the woman with Glen and Fionna.

The woman smiled warmly and greeted her sister with a hug.

"Well. I see you still know how to party," she said, holding Jasmin at arms-length to inspect her. "Are you hurt?"

Jasmin's mouth opened, but no words came out. She shook her head and regarded her sister with surprise. "Opal...what are you doing here?"

"You called me, remember. Something about an emergency with a friend of yours. I just arrived at your place about an hour ago. You weren't there so I used a locater spell to find you. Got here and it looked like World War III was going on inside. Ran into these two out back." She pointed her thumb at Fionna and Glen. "Decided to crash your little party. Glad we did."

"I'm glad you did as well."

Torie raced up to them. "Hey, I don't mean to intrude on this family reunion, but we should probably go after Elric and Max."

She started for the door, only to be stopped by Jasmin's grip on her jacket.

"Yeah, that would be a negative. They can handle themselves…and you're without any magic, in case you forgot."

Torie frowned. How could she forget? She might as well have hid in a closet for all the good she had been during the fight. She felt a pain in her right hand and looked down to see that she had a death grip on the white gem Jasmin had given her.

Fat lot of good it had been.

She shoved the stone into her pocket and was about to argue further when Max and Elric ran back into the bar, shifting to human.

"Wow. That is one fast hunter," said Elric.

"We followed her scent a couple hundred yards into the woods, then it just vanished. No idea where she went," Max said.

"You won't get a bead on her that way," said Opal, turning to face the wolves. "She's using divinity power to cloak herself. I could smell it on her as soon as I walked in."

Torie moved to stand next to Elric, grabbing his shoulders and spinning him around to face her. She threw herself into his arms before drawing back to take a close look at him.

"Are you okay?" she asked, giving him the once over for injuries.

"I am," he said, cocking his head to one side, not quite certain what to make of her concern.

"Um, I'm fine too," said Max, staring at the two of them.

"Yes, you are," said Opal playfully, her eyes taking in the big werewolf in a single floor-to-ceiling sweep.

"Opal," said Jasmin, taking her sister by the elbow, "thank you. You and Glen probably saved all of us. Let me introduce you to my friends." She motioned for them to come closer. "You've met Fionna and her wife Glen. This is Max and Elric. Max is the sheriff here in Singing Falls; and this is Torie. She's the friend I called you about."

Opal smiled, extending a hand to Glen and Fionna.

"Nice to meet you officially. I like the hardware." She nodded at the shotgun Glen had retrieved.

"Speaking of, when did you start carrying that?" asked Jasmin. "Not that I'm not thankful you have it. Just curious."

"I started carrying when I realized there are certain elements in the town that want to kill you. Well, that and the fact that I'm the only human running with a bunch of supernaturals; a girl's gotta find a way to protect herself."

Opal laughed admiringly. "Exactly. And for the record, magic is fine in some situations; but sometimes, you just gotta take a bitch to the streets old school style." She turned to Torie then. "So. You're the witch with no hexes. It's a pleasure to meet you. We'll have a lot to talk about later." She leaned in and gave Torie a kiss on her cheek.

She then turned her attention to the two wolves, looking them up and down. "Um-hm. Hello boys."

"Um, this is Elric and—" started Jasmin.

"Shhh," said Opal appreciatively. "Girl, they might as well be a biscuit and a plate of gravy, cos I just wanna sop one up with the other and eat them both." She snapped her jaws playfully in their direction before turning back to her sister. "I always did have a thing for werewolves. So, sis. What have you been up to for the past twenty years?"

Her voice was caring but tinged with the faintest trace of hurt as well.

"Why don't we call it a night and regroup in the morning," suggested Torie. "We can bring you up to speed on everything that's happened lately. Plus, I'm sure you two could use the time to get reacquainted. I assume you'll be staying with Jasmin?"

The sisters looked at one another before shrugging.

"I'll take that as a yes," said Torie. "Max, will you be taking final statements from everyone? Would you mind sharing those with us tomorrow?"

The wolf nodded and stepped away, heading for the kitchen where the staff had been gathering.

Opal looked around the room, taking in the damage that had been caused by the fisticuffs. She stopped as she took it all in, her attention locked on the booth Torie had singled out earlier. She walked over to it and stared, not moving until her sister and Torie walked up to her.

"What is it?" asked Jasmin.

"Something…not natural was sitting here," she said, running one hand lightly across the edge of the table.

"Do you know what it is?" said Torie, her breath nearly cut off by excitement. "Max said that there is literally nothing here…a blank spot that his senses can't register."

"Well, that's because his senses, sharp as they may be, are still grounded in the physical world. My senses come from the spiritual world. And whatever was sitting here… does not belong in this world."

Silence hung over the group until Opal suddenly pivoted to face them, a huge smile on her face.

"Oh well. Whatever it is, it's gone now. Jasmin, I'm starving. What say you and I go get something to snack on and then head back to your place. Torie, you're welcome to join us...that is unless you have something more pressing." She turned her head, taking in Elric in a glance.

Torie felt her face grow hot.

"Thanks for the offer. But I do have something pressing I need to attend to. Why don't you come over tomorrow?"

Opal nodded. "Absolutely. I'll need to examine you up close and personal, and it will go better in a space you're most comfortable in."

Torie wasn't exactly sure how she felt about that, so she just nodded, and then turned her attention to Elric.

"Can I get a lift home with you?"

"Of course," the wolf replied. "That would make me happy."

As they were leaving, Max entered the room and told everyone to stay alert and be careful.

"You as well," said Opal, her tone now very sombre. "Don't go after that hunter alone. She's armed with a type of magic you're not equipped to handle."

Max didn't reply. He looked in Elric's direction and gave him a single nod.

———————

The ride back to Torie's house was made almost in complete silence. She was thankful for the crunching of gravel as Elric turned into the long driveway that led to her home. At least the sound was something to fill the space between them.

"Here we are," he said, shifting into park but not turning off the car.

Torie moved to open her door but stopped. "Elric, can we talk? Not out here I mean, but inside."

He just nodded, quieted the engine and followed her to her porch. Once inside, Torie took their coats and hung them in the entry closet. The fire had gone out and without having to be asked, Elric went about adding wood and relighting it.

"Thank you," Torie said, rubbing her arms. Autumn days in the North Carolina mountains were beautiful, but once the sun went down, there was a pervasive chill that quickly reached through any nook or cranny it could find in order to settle into one's bones.

"Here," Elric said, retrieving a soft throw blanket from the back of the loveseat and draping it around her shoulders. "How's that?"

"Perfect," she said. "You always know what I need before I do."

He laughed lightly. "Well, not everything."

Torie gave him a half grin and asked him to sit next to her on the couch.

"Elric, I need to apologize to you. I've been such an ass to you lately. And that's wrong, especially to you of all people. I've just…I mean, everything that happened, I'm still trying to adjust."

The big wolf shook his head and threw an arm around her, pulling her close.

"You don't owe me anything, least of all an apology. What you've been through is something I can't even begin to fathom. You're entitled to process however you see fit."

"Maybe. But I'm not entitled to cut the people that are closest to me out of my life. I made the decision to give up my magic in order to save Wednesday's baby. And no matter how many times I play that night over in my head; I would still do the same thing again. I made that decision. Now I have to come to terms with the consequences."

Elric sat forward, twisting his body to face her. "But you don't have to come to terms with it alone."

Torie looked away, unable to hold his eyes.

"Torie, vulnerability is nothing to be ashamed of. We don't have to be afraid to reach out and take someone's hand. But I get it. Opening up is scary. Especially when you've been burned so badly once before."

Immediately she turned, her eyes taking in his face. "No. Don't say that. You are nothing like Ward. I don't compare you to him, so don't you do it either."

Elric smiled. "Well, that's good to know. But all I'm saying is I understand where you're at. We shared my body, Torie; literally. You think that was easy for me? I knew the enormity of allowing you inside my head. It was the ultimate extension of the mental rapport we shared."

"Yes, That's just it! Shared, as in past tense. Elric, I had no idea how natural the connection I had with you was. I didn't realize the extent of it until it was gone. Not just with you, but this place…this weird, wonderful little town I've grown to love. I can't expect you to just stay by my side based on powers I no longer possess."

And there it was. She had spoken the one thing she feared more than all else. Human Torie couldn't possibly be as interesting, as deserving of love by someone as amazing as this werewolf, as witch Torie had been. She took a deep breath and held it, wishing she could swallow the words she had just said.

Elric turned to her, his eyes searching hers. He didn't say

anything. At a time like this, words would have most likely failed him.

Instead, he gently placed the tips of his fingers under her chin and tilted her face up towards his. He leaned in slowly and kissed the top of her forehead, then the bridge of her nose, and finally, he sealed her lips with his own. His hand found the back of her head and lightly strummed her hair before finding its way down her shoulders to the small of her back where he pulled her body into his.

A spark became a flame, and a flame became an inferno inside of Torie. Her body ached and her heart sang as he lifted her off the couch.

No spells, no muttered incantations, no magic.

Just two bodies longing to know each other in the deepest, most primal way possible. She threw her arms around him, gripping him as strongly as she could as he carried her into the bedroom.

Chapter Seven

The setting autumn sun cast dappled shadows of orange and red that cascaded through the large window of the Tudor home that was nestled among the trees at the edge of a large, open meadow. The house sat atop a ridge that ran along the border of Singing Falls. It was far enough from town that tourists looking for hiking trails would never stumble across it, and those who lived in town would have no reason to venture too close unless they were invited.

Inside, a wood fire burned, giving off just enough warmth to make the vaulted living room feel cozy and less expansive.

Jasmin stood at the large, Wolf range, heating a kettle for coffee.

"You know, it's much quicker to heat water with magic," said Opal.

"Yes, I know. But I like the routine of making coffee this way. Magic shouldn't be used for everything."

Opal walked around the living room, stopping at the fireplace as she took in the photos that sat on the mantle.

They were pictures of Jasmin with Fionna, Taylor and Torie captured at various times over the past few months.

"Nice collection of pictures of your friends," she said.

Jasmin paused, aware of the emphasis that had been placed on the word friends. She continued taking cups out of the cabinets, not acknowledging the not-so-tiny dig her sister had sent her way.

"I can't help but notice that you don't have any pics of mama. Or me for that matter," she said, continuing her inspection of the room. There was a console table that sat behind the large, cream-colored couch that anchored the space. She ran a finger along the bric-a-brac that sat on the console.

Jasmin took a deep breath. "The photos I have of us as children are packed away. I only recently started putting out more personal artifacts."

That was a true statement she realized. For the most part, her home, immaculate as it was, was decorated with objects de art that she had purchased; but had little meaning for her on a personal level.

"What's the matter?" said Opal. "Ashamed of your family? Or are you trying to rid yourself of unpleasant memories?"

Jasmin didn't answer as she took the kettle of heated water and began the intricate process of creating a fresh pourover coffee for her sister. She let the cup sit as she went to the refrigerator to retrieve fresh cream, which she added to a small silver boat meant to keep it cold. She placed it on the center island of the modern kitchen and added a small canister of sugar in the raw.

"Do you want anything other than cream and sugar?" she asked of her sister.

"Hmm. Do you have any Baileys?"

Jasmin pursed her lips together. "You know, that does sound pretty good." She made her way to the refrigerator and took out an open bottle from the door.

Opal smiled. "Looks like we grew up with the same tastes."

Jasmin didn't answer, pouring a splash of the Irish liquor into the cups. She handed a cup to her sister and motioned for her to follow her out onto the deck. It overlooked a steep drop as the hillside on which her home was built dropped away. Beyond that, the canopy of the trees looked like a patchwork quilt of brilliant fall colors spread out before them. The deck was expansive, and at one end was a sitting arrangement complete with a coffee table with a gas fire pit built into its center.

Jasmin flicked a switch and blue-white flames shot upward, warming the immediate vicinity.

"So, I have to ask," said Opal, taking a sip of her coffee, "I mean, I know we have a lot to discuss, but this is serious and needs to be settled first." Her tone was deadly serious, and Jasmin found herself holding her breath. "You have to be honest with me here…are those wolves single? Cos, damn girl, they are fine! Or are they together? Cos you know I don't judge."

She erupted in laughter at the look on her sister's face.

"Oh loosen up, sis," she said. "But I'm kinda serious."

Jasmin rolled her eyes. "Max, the taller of the two, is single. As far as I know. Elric is spoken for."

"Ah yes. Let me guess…Torie?"

Jasmin nodded, sitting her coffee on the table as she shifted her weight to observe her sister. "Opal, thank you for coming here. You didn't have to; but I'm glad you did."

Opal squinted her eyes slightly. "What you mean to say is that I don't owe you anything."

Jasmin felt her cheeks grow hot. "You're right. You don't owe me anything."

"Do they know?" Opal asked. "About us I mean. What happened."

Jasmin took a deep breath. "I told Torie about it; well, most of it. Some things I'd rather not relive."

Opal said nothing as she gazed out over the foliage, watching the dying light settle across the landscape. They were high enough that the wind whipping through the trees was enough to hasten the chill in the evening air.

"It was terrible, that night. Even now, I still have nightmares about it. I...I still feel so—"

Jasmin cut her off, holding her hand in the air. "We don't need to relive that. It was bad for both of us."

"I'm surprised you called me. That just goes to show how much this woman means to you. I didn't think I'd ever hear from you again."

Jasmin felt her temples throb as she wrestled with her emotions. "If I've learned anything over the past few months, it's that nothing is guaranteed. Our time on this world is limited. I wanted to make peace with you while I still could; this thing with Torie just gave me a reason."

"I hate that you needed to find a reason. I'm sorry for that. Not a day goes by that I don't replay that evening in my mind. How stupid I was. How naive."

"Stop it, Opal," Jasmin said, forcing her sister to look at her. "We are not the girls we were back then. We've grown into the witches who are sitting here now. We both know that dwelling on the past solves nothing."

"You're right. It's just that looking back, with what I know now; I understand the folly of what I attempted. We were lucky to survive. And the whole time, when we were cowering at Gram's house, all I could think about was what if I had gotten you killed as well."

A tear slipped from her eye, rolling down her cheek.

"But you didn't," said Jasmin. "We both lived." She felt a heaviness pass between them. Yes, they both lived, but their existence had come at a heavy price. "Why did you leave the way you did? Not even a goodbye."

Try as she might, she couldn't quite contain the tiny bite of anger in her voice.

"I couldn't face you, Jas. I couldn't process what I had done. I killed our mother. I..." she choked up, her voice tearing within her throat, refusing to come out.

Jasmin reached over and wrapped an arm around her sister, pulling her close. Together, they cried. They cried until no more tears would come, and then they sat in silence and darkness, watching the shadows at play across the deck in the flicker of the firelight.

"I don't think we need to rehash the past anymore," said Jasmin, reaching up one hand to stroke her sister's hair. "We're here now and we have a lot to catch up on."

Opal sat up, wiping at her face. "Speaking of catching up, this place! It's beautiful, Jasmin. I take it the whispers about the hex witches living in this area are true. That you're all rich somehow."

"Well, I wouldn't say rich. At least I'm not. Some of the others...yes. This community is built on generational wealth being shared. Some of the witch families started a fund generations ago, and it's used as shared income for the lineage; it also pays for the town's needs. In my case, as you know, we had nothing. So nothing was contributed to the fund in my name. Torie, on the other hand...well, she's rich."

Opal frowned. "Then how do you afford all of this? Did

you come up with some kind of money spell? Cos you know that comes with consequences."

"No, nothing like that. I would never use magic for personal gain. I made some very wise investments years ago, and they have paid off. Big time."

"Oh cool. Let me guess…Apple? Microsoft?"

Jasmin shook her head, laughing. "Try bitcoin."

Opal nodded appreciatively. "Look at you, getting all crypto and making that money. Good for you."

"And what about you? What are you doing these days?"

"Oh, I run a small tarot and gift shop. I also sometimes help out the local police department in New Orleans with unsolved murders. They pay me a stipend to keep me on retainer. Being able to talk to spirits comes in handy in solving murders."

"And I take it you're single as well?" Jasmin asked.

"What? Why would you say that? You don't think I look like I could get someone?"

"No. I'm going by your questions regarding the were-wolves, silly."

Opal laughed. "Oh yeah. You're right. I'm as single as they come. But I kind of like it that way. What about you? Seeing anybody special?"

Jasmin shook her head. "No. No one to speak of."

Her voice trailed off in a way that told Opal not to press any further.

"It's not easy," Opal said, "being a witch and maintaining a relationship. Men aren't built for that kind of emotional support. At least not the non-supernatural ones." She winked knowingly at Jasmin, who in turn elbowed her playfully in the side.

"I think the thing I most missed about us not growing

into adulthood together is not being with you when we got our powers."

Opal nodded in agreement. "I thought about you a lot. Wondered what kind of witch you were becoming."

"Same here. But I guess that old fortune teller was right; you work spirit hexes?"

"Yes, that seemed to be my calling. I mean, I can work an incantation as well as the next witch, but the spirit world is where I feel most comfortable."

"I figured as much. That's why I called you. Do you think there is something you can do to help Torie get her hex powers back?"

"What is her specialty?" Opal asked.

"Not entirely sure. She's powerful...or at least she was. Her natural skill that developed was a form of telepathy; she could communicate with shifters while they were in their animal forms."

Opal arched an eyebrow. "That's different. Haven't heard of anyone who could do that. Did you know her mother as well? Was that a power she possessed?"

"Not that I am aware. She was powerful too; but more aggressive with her magic. She was a very powerful fire-hex master. Torie's magic seems more defensive in my opinion."

Opal nodded. "I'll need to give her a thorough once-over. Can you tell me how it happened? How she lost her power."

Jasmin recounted the events that led to Torie moving to Singing Falls and her recent encounter with the warlock.

When she finished, Opal just shook her head. "Warlocks. Nasty little men."

"Sounds like you've had a run-in with them before."

"I wish I could say I didn't, but yeah. Those unsolved murders? A couple of them involved warlocks."

"Do you think you can get her magic back, Opal?"

Her sister grasped her hand and gave it a squeeze. "I'm a witch doctor. If *I* can't, no one can."

The statement might have sounded pessimistic coming from anyone else, but Jasmin heard only positivity in her sister's voice, and it offered her hope; tiny as the sliver may have been.

"Okay, it's getting a little chilly out here," Opal said. "Let's go inside and have another cup of this coffee and Baileys. Only this time, let's leave the coffee out. Plus, we need to talk about that hunter who attacked you and your friends."

"I've heard of them, but she was actually the first one I've seen in action. She was scary as hell."

"Yeah, she was," agreed Opal. "But her afro-puffs were tight. Gotta give her that."

Jasmin laughed as they made their way inside. She was feeling much better now than she had at the beginning of the evening. Her sister would be able to help Torie.

She had to. Jasmin refused to accept anything else.

As they went back inside, a shadow detached itself from the blackness in the far corner of the deck where the light from the fire pit did not reach. It managed to slither inside the house, slipping through the door leading into the kitchen. Only Opal seemed to sense something, as she glanced over her shoulder, pausing slightly before following her sister through the house.

Chapter Eight

The next morning, Torie slept in without meaning to.

The smell of eggs and bacon frying, as well as the unmistakable aroma of fresh ground coffee wafting through the house, woke her stomach up before the rest of her.

She rolled out of bed and threw on her robe before making her way into the kitchen. She was greeted by the sight of Elric in a tee shirt and nothing else, his back to her as he tended the food on the range.

"Whoa...where are your clothes?" she asked, averting her eyes. "Nobody wants to be Donald Ducked first thing in the morning."

Elric frowned. "I don't get it."

"Donald Duck...the cartoon character famous for wearing a shirt and no bottoms? Never mind. Just go put something on. Who fries bacon with their delicate parts exposed anyway?"

He walked past her heading for the bedroom, and she gave him a playful slap on the rear.

"How's this?" he said, walking back in. He had retrieved his boxer briefs from the pile of clothing on the bedroom floor.

Torie had to admit she liked the sight. "Now I'm torn… maybe I did prefer you the other way."

Elric laughed and drew her close for a kiss. "I was hoping you would stay in bed. I wanted to surprise you."

"Oh, you surprised me enough in bed," she said with a smile. "You surprised me a couple of times if I remember right." She returned his kiss, the two hungers she felt rising within her. They parted, and she gave into the rumble in her stomach, plopping herself down at the island.

"Max called," Elric said, taking a plate he had set out and sliding a couple of eggs onto it for her. "He wants us to go back out and look for that hunter. He thinks she has to be in town. A couple of people told him they saw her arrive a couple of days ago."

Torie stared at his back until he turned to face her.

"You heard what Jasmin's sister said. She specifically said not to go after her."

"She told Max not to go after her alone. And he didn't. But with my help, it will be two against one."

"You mean like it was last night? When she didn't really have much of a problem wiping the floor with both of you; and that was with Jasmin helping."

"She caught us by surprise is all. Won't be so lucky next time."

Or the two of you won't be so lucky, Torie thought.

"She was very scary," said Torie. "So that's a hunter, huh?"

"Yep. And she wasn't so scary. We've fought them before and lived to tell the tale."

Torie wasn't sure she liked the way that sounded.

"So are you going to tell me why she was after you?" She reached over and took the cup of coffee he slid her way. "I mean, she actually mentioned the two of you by name and flat out said she came for you guys."

Elric shrugged and turned to dish his own plate.

"Uh uh. No sir," said Torie. "What were we talking about last night? Honesty? Being open and letting one another in?"

"You're right," he said after a pause. He placed his plate on the island and shoveled a forkful of eggs into his mouth. "I don't know who that hunter is, and that's the truth. But you're right; she was zeroed in on me and Max."

"Why?"

"If I had to guess, I'd say it has to do with some of the stuff we were involved in prior to our arrival here in Singing Falls. Remember how I told you we worked for some pretty shady people down in Trinity Cove?"

Torie nodded, reaching for more of the coffee.

"Well, my bet is it has something to do with the bosses we worked for. We were hired muscle back then. If our boss needed to scare someone, or they owed up on a debt and weren't able to pay…well our job was to go out and find a way to squeeze the money they owed out of them. Basically, we enforced his will. Crooked as it might have been at times."

His face was forlorn as he played with his food. Torie could see he was hurting and she toyed with the idea of telling him he didn't have to continue. But she knew from experience that letting go of things that hurt could be cathartic.

"We never hurt anyone; at least not anyone that didn't

deserve it. The people that entered into deals with our boss were not upper echelon types. They were typically involved in shady doings of their own and would borrow money to feed their dark work."

"So, what happened? Why did you leave?"

"We didn't leave. We ran. The boss wanted us to do a job that involved applying pressure to a particularly nasty fellow by the name of Simms. The problem was, the only thing Simms cared about was his daughter. Putting pressure on him meant...well, it was a line we wouldn't cross. There was a confrontation, and to make a long, gory story short, our boss ended up losing an eye. To Max's claws. We went on the run after that. No one came for us, however; we left everything we had worked for behind, including everything we had gotten paid. Max assumed the money we forfeited had bought us our lives.

"That or the boss was actually too afraid of us to try anything. He was actually lucky that all Max took from him was his eye."

Torie didn't speak. She reached for a small pot of jam and spread it across her toast.

"So, you think your old boss sent the hunter after you?"

He shrugged. "Wouldn't put it past him. He wouldn't have been able to do the job himself...but a hunter? That levels the playing field in his mind. That's serious muscle he was able to hire. It's also a big flex for him."

"What do you mean by a flex?"

"It increases his street credibility in the eyes of the other underworld bosses. Hunters are notoriously hard to employ. They operate by a very strict personal code related to their calling. They usually can't be bought."

"I guess everyone has a price," Torie said quietly.

"Well, I don't want you to worry about this. Like I said, Max and I will search her out and…we'll reason with her."

Torie wasn't sure what his definition of 'reason' was, but she was pretty sure it didn't match hers.

"How will you even find her? You said you could only track her so far in the woods and then her trail went cold."

"We'll find her. She has to be staying in town or close by."

Torie didn't respond, instead she sat there quietly, her eyes closed and back ramrod straight. To Elric, she seemed to be intent on hearing something far away. He tilted his head to the side, listening for whatever it might be that had captured her attention.

"What is it?" he asked.

Torie shook her head before opening her eyes and smiling at him. "I was just trying to see if I could hear your thoughts."

He didn't respond, but instead walked behind her and wrapped his strong arms around her, hugging her tight.

"What's it like for you?" he asked. "I kind of miss the feel of you rummaging around in my head."

She laughed. "You make it sound like I'm invading your space when you put it like that."

"Oh, I never minded. It was comforting; knowing you were so close to me, even when we weren't together."

"And now it's gone. Forever."

"No," he said. "That was one form of our connection. We will build new ones. Like last night. I have never felt closer to someone than I did to you."

Torie sighed and gave his arm a squeeze. "It was nice. I'd almost forgotten just how nice it can be."

She refused to dwell on anything other than what they had being a positive. She wasn't going to ask him if he were sure that he could accept her as she was; normal. She was who she was at this point, and if it wasn't good enough for anyone other than herself, then so be it.

"Hey, what about Jasmin's sister? Didn't you say that maybe she could help you?"

"Oh crap. What time is it?" she asked, glancing at the digital readout on the stove. "They're coming over this morning. I need to get dressed."

"You do that. I'm meeting Max in town."

Torie hesitated before drawing away from his embrace. "Elric, will you do me one favor? Will you at least hold off on trying to find this hunter? At least until I've had a chance to work with Jasmin's sister? I'd rather the two of you not go into this alone."

He was silent as he held her, rocking gently back and forth.

"I'll tell you what. I'll talk to Max and we'll just do some recon. See if maybe we can pick up her trail anywhere in town, try to get a bead on where she may be staying. But we won't confront her; not without backup. I'll promise you that, if you'll promise me something."

"Anything."

"If Jasmin and her sister can't get your powers back, you sit this one out."

Torie felt heat rising up her neck as she spun around to face him. "That's not fair."

"It absolutely is. You saw what this hunter could do. I don't want you involved if you don't have your magic for protection. If you can't promise me that, then Max and I will go it alone after her."

She was quiet as she contemplated his words. Of course he was right, and she mentally kicked herself for having to admit that. Over the past few months she had gotten used to magic. It had gone from being something scary and unknowable, to being a blessing. And not having it sucked because she had actually accomplished real good in her time in Singing Falls.

"Fine. I will sit this one out."

"Good," he replied, hugging her again, this time sniffing at her hair. "I want you safe."

"Same here, Elric. I feel safest with you at my side. So don't do anything stupid. And if Max wants to do something stupid…well that's on him. There is no shame in running away and leaving him if you have to."

Elric laughed as Torie nestled in against his chest. He kissed her gently on the top of the head and hugged her close. She smiled, breathing in his scent. For some reason, that had always annoyed her when Ward did it; the whole being kissed on the top of the head. For some reason it always felt dismissive when he did it. Like she expected him to follow it up with a swat on the rear as he ushered her from the room and told her to go play.

But when Elric did it, she felt warm and happy. Of course, the fact that he followed it up with a proper kiss that brought a shiver to her spine didn't hurt.

"I'll check in with you later," Elric said. He went into the bedroom to finish dressing, leaving Torie to finish her breakfast.

"Leave the dishes in the sink," he said as he passed back through, heading for the door. "I'll clean up later."

Once he was out of the house, Torie hopped into the shower and dressed. She wasn't sure what to expect with Jasmin's sister, but it was all she could do to calm her nerves. Why had she had that extra cup of coffee? Her nerves were firing on all cylinders now.

She checked her watch just as there was a knock on the front door.

"Took you long enough," she said, swinging it open.

The young woman standing on her front porch was most definitely not Jasmin or her sister.

"Well," said the hunter, "I had to wait for your pet to leave. Mind if I come in?"

Chapter Nine

Torie stared at the young woman with the afro puffs, dressed in leather, with one hand casually draped across the hilt of her knife.

"I'm not a vampire," said the hunter, "I really don't need your permission to enter. But I like to think I have manners."

Torie nodded cautiously and stepped aside. The woman walked in slowly, looking around the expansive living room she had just entered.

"Nice place. Large, but still feels lived in; almost homey."

Torie closed the door behind her and walked over to the fireplace. Her mind was spinning, but she never took her eyes off the young woman, who flopped herself down onto the couch and lazily stretched her legs out, resting her feet on the coffee table.

"Please don't do that," Torie said, her voice trembling slightly.

"Don't do what?"

"Put your feet on the furniture like that. Sorry, but if you're practicing your manners, then that's one to add to your list."

The hunter frowned before slowly placing her feet back onto the ground. "I hadn't heard you weren't supposed to do that. People do it all the time where I'm from. And on the television as well."

"Yeah, well that's something that makes me crazy when I see it on TV," Torie said. "Especially when someone climbs onto the bed with their shoes on. Makes me wonder if they were raised in a barn."

She saw something click in the hunter's eyes, but the young woman didn't respond. Just continued to look around.

Without taking her eyes off her, Torie positioned her body towards the iron poker that stood propped against the fireplace mantle.

"Oh I wouldn't," said the hunter, without making eye contact. "Trust me when I say, I could snap your arm before you could even make a move to grab that." She then rolled her head in Torie's direction and locked her with a look.

A look that said she wasn't joking.

"What do you want?" Torie asked.

"Well, what I wanted was the two wolves. I mean, don't get me wrong, I'll still get them; but this town has presented me with something else I now want as well."

"And what might that be?"

The hunter stood up, walking around the couch to the console table behind it. She leaned down, studying the array of pictures displayed.

"That's not your concern," she said, running her fingers across the top of the frames. "But if what you meant to ask me was what do I want *here*, in this house, well that I can

73

answer." She walked up to Torie, standing close enough that she made Torie even more nervous than she already was. "I want some information from you."

"Information? About what? I'm new here in town…I don't know anything."

"New? Maybe. Ignorant? No. You know that you're sleeping with a werewolf, don't you?"

"Oh, that's ridiculous…my boyfriend is—"

The hunter cut her off. "Don't. Don't play dumb. You were at the bar the other night with the whole gang. You know perfectly well what he is. But what I want to know is why would a human like yourself be hanging out with a cadre of supernaturals?"

Torie didn't answer, swallowing hard. Her throat felt like it was drier than the Sahara.

"At first I thought maybe you were one of them. But then, none of my divinity objects registered you as anything more than human." She spun on her heel and walked away, heading for the kitchen. "So, I'm just curious; what is your connection to the supernaturals?"

"I…They're just my friends. It's no big deal who or what they are. This town, this community, is built on acceptance."

"Yeah, I kinda noticed that. Never seen anything like it honestly. Of course, from what I've seen, not all the humans know what the other half of the town is." She stopped walking and turned back to Torie, placing her index finger on her lips as a thought struck her. "But that works both ways. I've also noticed most of the supernaturals don't know what some of the humans are into either."

Torie wasn't sure what to make of that, and she wasn't sure how much to ask. The hunter saw the look of bewilderment on her face and smiled.

"See, I thought maybe you were one of those humans. That's why I needed to know what I was dealing with."

"What are you talking about? What do you mean by other humans?"

The hunter shrugged. "Not important. You're obviously not one, so it doesn't matter. But I do need you to tell me what you know about the two witches. The ones from the bar."

Torie felt a line of sweat break down her back.

"They're just friends, like I said. They keep to themselves. I don't really know that much about them, personally. I met them through El— my boyfriend."

"Elric. You can say his name. I already know it and that of his old alpha's as well." She walked to the far side of the island and rested her hands on the granite. Then she leaned in, supporting her weight on the island. "And something about what you just said wasn't entirely true, was it?"

Torie swallowed hard but didn't break eye contact with the hunter. "What I said was the truth. Honest it was."

The hunter cocked her head to one side before moving around the island to the side where the stove was. She ran her hand over the large butcher block where the knives were housed. She smiled as her hand came to rest on the handle of the larger butcher knife.

"See…there it was again. That little something that tells me you aren't being truthful. You know, telling when someone is lying is a talent I have; well, one of many. It comes in handy in my line of work."

"Which is?" Torie asked.

The hunter laughed. "I help people recover things they lost…or things that maybe ran away from them. And in running away, they may have taken something that didn't belong to them. When that happens, I go get it back; and deal with the thieves however my boss tells me to."

"And who is your boss?"

"The one with the fattest check book, of course."

"You're a mercenary then? And let me guess, your boss put a price on Elric and Max's head, right?"

"Something like that."

"And it doesn't bother you? That maybe you're working for someone that is just using you to get what they want?"

"Hey, a girl's gotta eat, right?" She looked around the well-appointed kitchen and waved her hand. "We can't all be loaded."

Whether she meant to or not, her words gave Torie an idea.

"If all you're doing this for is money, then let me make you an offer. Whatever your boss is paying you to do this, I'll double that to walk away now; without hurting anyone."

"It doesn't work that way."

"But it could. I can pay you enough that you can go anywhere you want; start over again, and no one would be the wiser."

"I'd know. I've never failed at delivering on a contract. Don't think I'll start now."

Torie's mind was racing. "Do you like what you do? It doesn't seem like the kind of life that has a future."

The hunter looked at her, brows furrowed. "What? You mean because I don't have a 401K or stock options? Is that how you measure satisfaction in a job? Is that what got you all of this?"

Torie hesitated before answering. "No. I inherited this from my mother."

The hunter stopped and stared at her. "Well, aren't you

special. You know what I inherited from my mother? Jack shit."

Her clenched fists told Torie that a nerve had been struck. She held up both hands to the hunter.

"Hey, I'm sorry. I didn't mean to upset you. Honestly, I didn't have the best relationship with my mother. That was why I moved here…to get reacquainted with her after my marriage fell apart."

"Yeah, well that's all fine and good for you. But it's not a possibility with my mother. She tossed me out of her life after I was born. So there won't be any happy family reunions coming up, I can guarantee you that."

"So you, what, raised yourself?"

"Don't be ridiculous. Of course not. But if you're trying to get me to open up about my childhood, forget it. That's not what I'm here for. I want to know what your connection is to the witches and the wolves. And don't lie to me again." She took the large carving knife from its resting place and laid it on the island in front of her.

Torie looked around. She had no doubt that she couldn't get to a weapon in time to put up a fight. Even if she could, what would she be able to do? She'd seen the hunter toss around werewolves like they were stuffed animals.

Before she could respond, the sound of the front door flying open and footsteps running through the living room hit her ears.

Jasmin and Opal burst into the room. A blue orb of magic encircled Jasmin's fists, and Opal's eyes glowed white as ghostly tentacles swirled about her.

The hunter snatched up the knife in front of her and turned to face them, a smile on her face. She glanced at Torie, who had moved to stand behind her friends.

"So, you're still claiming that you have nothing to do with them?" the hunter said. "They just happen to come running to your rescue?" She stepped out from behind the island cautiously, reaching into her belt to withdraw a second knife.

"You need to leave before things get ugly," said Jasmin, not taking her eyes off the hunter.

"Your magic won't work on me, witch. I'm protected against it."

"Yes, I noticed that when we were at the bar," said Opal, stepping forward. "But I'm betting you aren't protected against physical attacks. My magic is a little more subtle than that." The phantom tentacles began to flare outward, striking at the hunter like snakes as Opal mentally commanded them to inch toward the young woman.

"Plus," said Jasmin, "we brought back up."

The back door opened slowly, and Fionna and Glen entered. Glen leveled the familiar shotgun in the hunter's direction, one finger curled lightly around the trigger.

The hunter didn't move as they advanced on her. "I'm betting I can get to you before you can pull that trigger."

"Oh yeah?" said Glen, her tone flat and menacing. "Why don't you mess around and find out?"

"Okay, stop," said Torie, stepping forward from behind Jasmin and Opal. "There will be no fighting in this house. Glen, put that thing away before you blow my cabinets up. And you two," she turned to Opal and Jasmin, "power down. Before you all came busting up in here, we were in the middle of a conversation."

Jasmin turned to her friend, her face dropping.

"A conversation? She was holding a knife on you!"

"I wasn't going to use it," said the hunter. "It was just for show. Mostly."

"My offer still stands," said Torie. "Double."

The hunter was staring at Jasmin as she slowly made her way past them and into the living room.

"You know my answer to that. Besides, I got what I came here for."

Torie frowned. "What are you talking about?"

The hunter slowly placed her knife back in its sheath and then withdrew her golden chain. "I'm walking out of here, witch," she said to Jasmin. "And if you try and stop me, someone is going to get hurt. Bad." She glanced back at the others, leveling a look at Glen before turning her attention back to the two witches. "Don't worry. I'll be seeing you. Soon."

She turned to face Torie and smiled. "Just as soon as I skin your boyfriend."

With that, she sprinted for the door just as Opal sent one of her tentacles flowing at her. It just missed, grabbing air as the lithe hunter cartwheeled through the open door. As soon as her feet touched the porch, she vaulted into the air in a spin that carried her far enough from the house that Opal wouldn't have been able to reach her.

She sprinted for the road and was out of sight before those in the house had even made their way to the front door.

Torie let out a breath that felt like she had been holding in since the hunter stepped through her front door. She bent over, placing her hands on her knees.

"You okay, Torie?" asked Fionna, rushing to her side.

"I will be. As soon as my heart returns to its normal pace. I think I need some water."

Fionna helped her to the couch where she sat down, holding her head in trembling hands. Glen was at her side with a glass of water.

"Easy, don't gulp it," she said.

Torie sipped the water, looking up to see Opal and Jasmin still standing near the door.

"Did you manage to do it?" said Jasmin.

"No. She must have some other charm or something that blocked it," replied Opal.

"What? What did you try to do?" asked Fionna.

Jasmin walked into the living room where everyone else was clustered around Torie.

"Opal was hoping to put a magical tracker on the hunter."

"So that's why you were okay with her just waltzing out of here?" said Glen.

Jasmin nodded. "I have a feeling that hunter is in town for more than just Max and Elric. We need to know what she's up to."

"You're right," said Torie. "She said as much to me."

"What else did she say?" questioned Opal.

"Hey, let her relax and get her breath," said Jasmin. "She's lucky she wasn't hurt."

"No time to relax," said Opal. "She needs to tell us everything that was said while it's still fresh in her mind. Even the smallest details." She was looking at Torie and nodding.

"I really didn't get much out of her. She wanted to know what my connection was to the two of you and to Max and Elric. She couldn't understand why I would be friends with you."

"Why would she care about that?" asked Glen.

"Exactly," said Opal. "If she were only looking to kill the wolves, why hasn't she already done that? Something tells me she is more than a match for the two of them."

"Maybe she's one of those hunters who believes all

supernatural creatures are evil and need to be purged from the world," said Jasmin. "Maybe after the bar fight, she's looking to probe our weaknesses as well?" She looked from Opal to Fionna and finally back to Torie.

"I didn't get the feeling it was like that," said Torie. "Though she definitely wanted to know about the two of you."

"Did you tell her that you used to—that you are a witch as well?" asked Jasmin.

Torie shook her head. "No. She said that her..." she scrunched up her face trying to remember, "something she had, some kind of objects, registered me as human. That was what kept throwing her off. She couldn't understand why a human would be so close with witches and shifters. I told her that you were friends with my mother and that was how we got to know each other."

Jasmin nodded. "That's good. Hunters don't know how witch lineage works. She wouldn't have made the connection that you are a witch as well. That keeps you off her radar."

"What were you saying about an offer?" asked Opal.

Torie told them about the conversation she had with the hunter, about how she had tried to pay her off.

"Yeah, that won't work," said Jasmin. "They are way too wrapped up in some weird honor system that compels them to eradicate evil from the land, or something like that."

"I don't know," said Torie. "I get the feeling this one is not like that. She wants something. I think I was close to getting it out of her."

"Anything else you two talked about?" said Opal.

Torie started to shake her head, but then stopped, her eyes lighting up.

"No, there *was* something else! She said that the super-naturals in town didn't know what they were dealing with when it came to certain humans. Or something like that. She made it seem like some of the humans in town were hiding secrets of their own...secrets that could hurt the supernatural community."

"Interesting," said Opal. "Something tells me I'm going to like this little town."

"Hey, how did you know I was in trouble?" Torie asked.

"Magical security system, remember?" said Jasmin. "The wards I erected let me know the minute she crossed the threshold into your house."

"Oh yeah, I forgot about those."

Jasmin walked over to the coffee table and picked up the white gem she had given Torie. "Looks like that wasn't the only thing you forgot. I told you to keep this on you at all times."

Torie could only blush as she took the stone from her friend and slipped it into her pocket.

"So, what now?" asked Fionna. "Looks like reasoning isn't getting us anywhere with this hunter. What's the next step?"

"Well, there are two steps," said Jasmin, looking at her sister.

"First, we get Torie her magic back," said Opal.

"Second, we track this hunter down before she can do any more damage and run her out of town. For good," added Jasmin. She was about to say something else, but her phone began buzzing in her jacket pocket. She took it out, a frown crossing her face as she read the messages.

"What is it?" asked Torie.

"It's from Max," she said. "He and Elric found out something interesting. They were finally able to speak with the injured bus boy from the bar. The one who waited on the mystery woman that seems to be at the scene of each incident. He said it was Myra Simms. She's a school teacher at the high school. She was there with her husband."

"Wait a minute," said Glen. "Did you say Simms? Myra Simms and her husband Marcus?"

Jasmin shrugged. "He didn't send the name of the husband. Why?"

Glen shook her head in disbelief. "Because that's not possible. I was Marcus's nurse at the hospital. He died six months ago."

Chapter Ten

No one said anything. They all stared at Glen, letting her words sink in.

"Wait, are you sure?" asked Jasmin.

"Of course I'm sure," Glen replied. "I literally sat at the man's bedside, holding his hand when he passed. He suffered from lung cancer, but it was in remission. Myra had left town for a teachers' seminar in Raleigh. Marcus developed a blood clot that traveled to his lungs while she was away and was brought into the hospital for emergency surgery. I was the nurse anesthetist on duty. The surgeon tried everything, but he didn't make it; I watched him breathe his last breath. I didn't see Myra when she finally arrived at the hospital, but I heard she was devastated by the loss.

"So, unless she has gotten over that and remarried in the past couple of months; whoever was with her at that bar could not have been her husband."

Torie looked around excitedly. "This has to be connected to the wave of violence that seems to have broken out in Singing Falls. We need to talk to this Myra Simms." She stood up and started to head for her bedroom at the back of the house.

"Whoa there, missy. Where do you think you're going?" demanded Jasmin.

Torie narrowed her eyes. "I'm going with you to follow up on this."

"Oh, I don't think so," said Jasmin. "You're staying right here with me and Opal. Or did you forget why we were coming over?"

Torie broke eye contact, crossing one arm across her body and chewing lightly on her lower lip. "Why don't we do that after we get back?"

Opal and Jasmin exchanged looks before Jasmin moved to the sofa and sat down. She patted a seat next to her.

"Come here, honey," she said softly. Reluctantly, Torie sat down beside her. "Are you afraid to work with us on this? It might be a chance to get your magic back."

Torie sighed, blinking back tears.

"That's just it," she said. "Those two words, 'might' and 'chance'…they don't sound very definitive. I'm just not sure I want to get my hopes up and then I end up right back where I am now."

Opal smiled and reached for Torie's hand. "There are no definites, Torie. But what I can say is that I will definitely try my best to help you. When we are done, I can say with confidence that everything possible was done to help you. But you have to be a willing participant in this. It has to be a two way street."

Torie looked at her and nodded. "Okay. Fine, I'll do whatever it takes. But we can't just sit on this lead. I mean, that hunter mentioned that humans were doing things in the community that we weren't aware of. What if this is related?"

Jasmin nodded. "I agree. That's why I'm going to ask Fionna and Glen to go into town and find Elric and Max." She turned to the shifter and her wife to address them directly. "I want the four of you to split up. Two go and see if you can track down this Myra Simms and see what you can get out of her. The other two, come back here. I have a feeling we are going to need some help with what Opal has planned." She glanced at her sister in a way that told Torie the two of them had been conspiring on something that neither was ready to discuss.

"We can do that," said Fionna. "We'll be careful, I promise." She leaned down and gave Torie a quick kiss on her cheek. "Good luck, Torie."

As they left the house, Torie felt a measure of relief wash over her. She didn't like the thought of Max and Elric out looking for that hunter. At least this way they wouldn't be alone.

When they were alone, the three witches sat in silence for a moment before Torie cleared her throat and spoke up.

"So, Opal, have you run into this type of thing before?"

"Not at all. I've never heard of a witch losing their powers. I didn't think it was possible; even if they hexed their own powers away."

"Then how are you going to help me?" Torie inquired.

"Well, when it comes to witches and injuries, I examine their aura and their spirit first. That's typically where the damage shows up. Then, I work on developing a healing ritual to fix what's broken."

"How do witches injure themselves?" Torie asked.

"Oh, there are all kinds of ways. Usually it's the result

of another witch; one hexes the other, or they are injured in a duel sometimes."

"I didn't know that," said Jasmin. "Witches fighting witches?"

"Battle magic is a real thing," said Opal. "Duels usually happen when one witch has something the other wants. Typically, it's all for show. Witches don't like to go up against one another...you never know when one will pay the ultimate price for such foolishness; so they like to show off, creating larger and larger spectacles of magical display until one backs down. But every now and then you see ones who took it a little too far and end up seriously hurting one another."

"And that's when they call the witch doctor," said Jasmin playfully.

Opal frowned. "I don't really care for that term in the way you mean it. I'm a witch, same as you. I just focus more on the healing arts and the spiritual side of magic."

"Sorry. Didn't mean to hit a nerve," said Jasmin. "You always were sensitive."

"And why is that a bad thing?" asked Opal.

"Didn't say it was," Jasmin replied, chancing a look and a wink at Torie.

Watching the banter back and forth between the two sisters, Torie found herself becoming more relaxed. She even broke a smile at some of the barbs they were throwing at one another.

"You two sound like you haven't been apart for a day," Torie said, "much less a couple of decades."

They both looked at her and then one another. Silence fell over the room again as Opal excused herself. She left the house and returned shortly thereafter with a large duffel bag. She unzipped it and sat it on the coffee table.

"Tools of the trade," she said, rummaging around in the bag. She pointed to the couch. "I need you to lay there and not move."

She took out a large, jagged, opaque crystal. Then she removed a bunch of leafy, green plants that were bound in a thin, silver wire.

"Is that sage?" asked Jasmin. "It smells like sage, but something else I'm not familiar with as well."

"It's a strain of sage crossed with hemlock."

"Isn't that poison?" said Torie.

Opal shrugged. "In the wrong hands, probably. But don't worry. I know what I'm doing. Plus, spirits can't resist this stuff."

"Wait, I thought you were going to look at *her* spirit," said Jasmin. "Not summon others."

"Hopefully it won't come to that. But better to be prepared. Now, I need one more thing. Something personal to you that has not been exposed to the spirit of anyone else."

Torie thought hard. "Does it have to be associated with positivity?"

"Not really. As long as it was yours and not polluted by another."

Torie excused herself and left the room. She went to the bedroom before returning with her fist closed around something. Holding out her hand, she opened it to reveal a gold wedding band with an emerald cut diamond.

"Wow," said Jasmin appreciatively.

"Looks like someone liked it and decided to put a ring on it," said Opal, nodding her head at the ring. "That's gotta be a couple of carats."

Torie didn't say anything, just handed it over to the witch.

"Will it do?" she asked.

Opal nodded. "Good or bad, I'm sure there is a lot of attachment to this. So yes, it will work. Now, lay down on the couch."

Torie did as she was asked, staring up at the ceiling as she tried to calm her nerves.

"Have you ever done any guided breathing?" asked Opal.

"No, I haven't. I mean, I've done some focused yoga breathing but that's about it. Is that the same thing?"

"Kind of. As we get older, more and more crap weighs on our minds. Things we would have brushed off in our youth now occupy land in the old gray matter. It can get heavy up there, and that can translate to spiritual and physical heaviness."

"Oh, and here I thought it was all the scones at Jim's Bakery," said Jasmin.

Opal shushed her sister. "That heaviness creates a sluggishness in one's aura. That can, over time, create a blockage in a witch's ability to perceive and manipulate the energies around them."

"Do you think that's what's happened to me?" asked Torie.

"We will find out. It's a good place to start at least. But in order for me to get the best look possible at your aura I need you to calm your thoughts. That will calm your body. I want you to close your eyes and do some box breathing. Take in a slow, deep breath for a count of six, hold that breath for a count of six, breathe out for a count of six and then rest for a six count before repeating. Got it?"

Torie nodded and closed her eyes. She started the breathing, focusing on the six count in her mind. She felt a heaviness rest on her stomach and realized Opal had rested the white crystal on her belly button. It should have been uncomfortable, but instead it helped to center her; giving her something else to focus her mind on. She could hear Opal tell her to relax and concentrate on her breathing; feel the breath come in through her nose, travel down her body and fill her lungs.

It was relaxing on a level Torie had never experienced before. She knew the warmth she felt spreading across her body was not just from her breathing.

She sensed the touch of magic. But was it all from Opal or did she dare hope that some of it might be hers?

"Uh-uh," said Opal, "keep your mind on your breathing. That's all you need to think about right now."

Torie swallowed and did as she was asked, trying her best to banish thoughts of magic from her mind. She heard Opal start to whisper a chant. It was in a language she had heard Jasmin speak on occasion. What had she once called it? The language of hexes…that was it. She needed to learn it, she realized. Maybe it was another form of magic she could…

"Open your eyes," said Opal.

Torie felt like she had been drifting far away, and the sound of the witch's voice snapped her back into her body.

"What happened?" she asked. She felt confused and foggy, like she had been deep in sleep. "That was fast."

"Fast?" said, Jasmin. "You've been snoring for almost three hours."

Torie sat bolt upright, her eyes wide. She looked at her watch and then around the room, her face a mask of bewilderment and shock.

"Three hours? That's not possible. I barely closed my eyes."

"You also barely snored," said Jasmin, half to herself.

"What was that?" said Torie.

"I said you must have been tired out of this world," Jasmin said, a large smile breaking across her features.

Torie frowned and cast her eyes at Opal. "So? What did you find out?"

"Well, there is absolutely nothing wrong with you as far as your aura is concerned." She went about placing the crystal back in her bag in a nonchalant, methodical way.

"Wait, so that's it? No problem with my aura to explain what's going on?"

"Well fat lot of good you were," said Jasmin. She placed her hands on her hips and glared at her sister. "I'm pretty sure you just sat there waving your hands over her and mumbling for a few hours. I could have done that."

"Perhaps," said Opal. "But could you have divined that not only is her aura not disturbed, but that there is no residual magic remaining within her at all? She has no spark of the hex present...even in a dormant form. That's something I can work with."

Torie and Jasmin exchanged questioning looks.

"How is it a good thing if she has no trace of magic at all within her?" questioned Jasmin.

Torie looked at them, her eyes welling with tears. She had managed to remain slightly hopeful, but now, she didn't even attempt to hide the waves of despair that were threatening to crash down on her.

Opal held up a hand to her, imploring her to hold on just a bit longer. "Don't give up just yet. Like I said, I can work with empty. Had I found that you still had bits of magic still locked within you, and your aura was in perfect shape, that would have been disastrous. Very hard to put you back together after something like that. But you... you're empty. You purged all the magic from your being at a level I would not have thought possible."

"That would explain why you couldn't use the gems I gave you," said Jasmin.

Opal nodded. "Magic is a form of energy. And like all forms of energy, it can't be created or destroyed. You sent your magic away, Torie. That means we have two options to get it back."

She paused and went about rummaging in her bag yet again.

Jasmin was tapping her foot in annoyance. "Well, are you going to tell us those options?"

"The first is that we can ask the Elders to return your magic to you," said Opal.

"Elders? What Elders?" asked Jasmin.

"Our ancestors, dear sister. And by our, I mean all witches. When we cross over, part of our essence joins with the great collective...the spirits that guide and give us our birthright magic. Ah, this is what I was looking for." She took a long, slender thread of silver from her purse. It sparkled with power, lighting up the living room. She unwound the shiny cord, revealing it was roughly six feet in length. On either end was a small ring.

"What is that for," asked Torie, eying the mystical rope with caution.

"We'll need it to stay together where we're going," replied Opal.

"And just where is that?" said Jasmin.

Opal flashed her sister a large smile. "Through the veil, into the astral plane. It's the only way to get to the Elders and ask them to restore Torie's powers."

Jasmin's eyes widened. "You mean…are you saying, we're going to visit the spirit world of the dead?"

Opal's smile widened. "Buckle up, buttercup. It's about to get bumpy up in here."

Chapter Eleven

"Wait a minute," said Torie. "Hold up. We're going to do a…what…reverse seance?"

"Yes! Exactly," said Opal. "For something this big we need to go to the spirits. Not bring them to us. We have to ask them to give your powers back to you again. There's no way we would have the power to bring them to this plane, so we have to venture to them."

Jasmin was frowning and chewing at her lower lip. "Have you done this before, Opal?"

Her sister shrugged. "In theory."

Torie's eyes grew to the size of small saucers. "In theory? The hell does that mean?"

"It means that while the nature of my magic allows me to commune with the spirits, I've never actually walked among them; at least not on their turf."

Jasmin folded her arms. "So you pick now to try?"

Opal sighed. "What choice do we have?"

"You said there were two options," said Torie. "What's the other."

Opal frowned. She appeared to be on the verge of saying something but then decided not to.

"You're going to have to trust me. Let's try this. I really think it is our best option." She leveled her sister with a look. "You called me here because you knew, deep down, that I was her best shot at getting her powers back. Well, you were right. But you're going to have to trust me to do this my way. Okay?"

The silence in the room was heavy, weighing oppressively on the three of them. Finally, Torie nodded.

"Alright, I'm in. It's not like I have anything else to lose at this point."

Opal clapped her hands in glee. "Goody. Now, we just need one last thing before casting the spell. Can one of you text a couple of your friends and ask them to come back? Preferably the one with the big gun."

"Why?" asked Torie.

"Because while we journey into the astral plane, our physical bodies will be vulnerable in this world. And I rather like the idea of a big-ass gun watching over us than a couple of hot-headed wolves. Besides, your feelings for the one werewolf are too strong. His presence would be a distraction to your astral self."

Torie wasn't exactly sure what she meant, but she nodded, taking out her phone and calling Fionna's number.

Thirty minutes later, Fionna and Glen were standing next to them in the living room.

"Did you find the Simms?" asked Torie.

"We didn't get a chance to," said Glen. "Max was acting very weird. He kept having little freakouts about things. He kept saying he smelled very bad magic…so bad that he kept shifting in and out of his wolf form, which was creeping me out. He tracked the smell of magic to this area just outside of town. He stepped in some mud and completely lost it for some reason. Like he'd never seen mud before."

This got Opal's attention. "Mud? What color was it?"

"Not sure. The lighting down there wasn't the best," said Glen. "But I think it was gray."

Opal didn't say anything, focusing on the silver cord she was holding instead.

"What is it?" said Jasmin. "Does that mean something to you?"

"Maybe. But first things first. We need to focus on the journey we are about to undertake."

She motioned for Jasmin to sit on one end of the couch and for Torie to sit next to her. Then, she took a seat on the opposite side of Torie so that the two sisters were like book-ends to her. She slipped one ring at the end of the cord over her wrist, then passed the other ring to her sister. She instructed Torie to wrap the middle portion of the cord around both of her own wrists. Once they were all entangled in the binding silver, Opal closed her eyes and whispered to the braid, causing it to flare briefly before settling back down to its normal warm, white light.

"Okay. I have enchanted this silver thread. It will bind us together in the astral plane. Just don't pull free from it," Opal said, looking at Torie.

"Why would I do that?" Torie responded.

"No idea. I'm just saying, stay with us. No matter what you think you see, don't engage anything once we are across the veil. Things aren't what they seem. Jasmin, focus your magic on keeping us protected from anything that might want to try and hitch a ride. I'll do all the talking once we reach the elders. No matter what, don't speak to them unless they speak to you first; and if they do, answer their questions directly without trying to espouse on anything. Got it?"

They both nodded in response.

"Okay. Sit back, close your eyes, and don't focus on anything in this physical realm."

"Um, what do we do?" asked Fionna. "Anything in particular we should know about?"

"No. I just don't want our bodies left unguarded with a hunter in the area," said Opal.

"What if she shows up?" said Glen, her voice nervous and unsteady.

"Shoot first, worry about asking questions later," said Opal, fixing her with a hard stare.

Glen nodded, looking anxiously at her wife.

Then, the three witches settled back into the couch and closed their eyes. Opal raised her hands, lifting the silver thread into the air as she began to chant.

"Ancient spirits of those before,
providers of the power I now implore,
hear my plea, through the Soul of Wells,
and grant us audience behind your veil."

Immediately, the three witches went limp, each slouching over, their heads resting peacefully to one side, their breathing barely perceptible. Glen and Fionna exchanged worried looks before settling into the chairs opposite the couch.

For Torie, the feeling she experienced was the same as she had felt years ago when she had agreed to ride the Cyclone rollercoaster at Bush Gardens with her son. The ride promised the fastest acceleration of any ride on the planet; from zero to over sixty-five miles per hour. It had certainly lived up to its billing; rocketing the two of them up an incline at a dizzying speed. That was the ride that cemented Torie's fear of rollercoasters, and she had sworn she would never step foot on one again.

What she felt now was that times a thousand. She felt like she had been snatched out of her body and fit into a slingshot that flung her towards a black sky with an explosion of light showering her from behind. Had it been possible, she would have screamed; but as it was, she could barely breathe, let alone form sentences.

Everything around her was comprised of shades of gray and black. There was no up or down, left or right. She couldn't feel anything around her, and with no way to orient herself, to make sense of things, her mind was sending signals of fight or flight—and her body was definitely in the flight mode.

"It's alright," said a calming voice. It was Opal, and her tone was a soothing balm to Torie's racing mind. "We're on the astral plane right now, the meeting place of the spirits. Focus on my voice and calm yourself. Everything is okay. We've been granted an audience with the elders."

Torie focused on the sound of Opal's voice as it echoed in her mind. Slowly, she felt herself begin to calm down, although the disorientation she felt was something she couldn't explain. It was like having all her senses but no longer having a body to temper and guide them. That was when she realized that was exactly what had happened to them. Their essence had been ripped out of their bodies and deposited here.

Is this what if felt like to be dead, she found herself wondering.

That was too macabre a thought to allow free reign in her mind; especially in a place occupied by spirits. Could spirits read minds? If they could, what would they think if they heard what she—

"Torie! Snap out of it. Focus on the here and now." This time it was Jasmin who spoke to her mind.

Torie took the mental equivalent of a deep, cleansing breath and focused on her friends. She felt a weight around her, pulling at her, and instantly felt more at ease when she realized it was the silver thread Opal had wound around her. At least she couldn't float away into the nothingness. She tried to look around, slowly becoming aware that she could make out vague shapes in the swirling fog. Something, or some things, were flitting in and out of her periphery.

"We're here," said Opal. Torie had not been aware they were floating forward until she experienced the strange sensation of not moving. They were in one place now, and directly in front of her, Torie could make out another, much larger shape.

No. Not one shape. Three.

There were three enormous chairs sitting in front of them, and seated on each chair was an equally enormous figure. Each form was misty and dark, seeming to fade from view the harder she tried to focus on them. They were slender with flowing robes of green and black that swirled like fog about them. Featureless faces capped with wild growths of gray hair floating in all directions around them.

"Elders," said Opal, her tone that of deference and respect. "We thank you for granting your daughters an audience."

"Why have you sought us out, little one?" The voice, while singular, seemed to emanate from all three at once. In

Torie's mind it was less a voice and more a primal wail that she somehow understood.

"We come seeking a favor from you, most exalted ancestors."

A sigh from the ages-old witches seemed to roll through Torie, causing her astral form to ripple.

"You can dispense with the formality, young one. We are not royalty after all. Simply tell us what it is that has brought you here."

"I bring a friend, elders; one who has lost her place among us. She is a witch who no longer possesses the power to hex. I—we—would ask that you see fit to grant her the return of her powers."

There was a rumbling that passed through them, one that seemed to carry with it a million words, all spoken at the same time, yet Torie could comprehend none of them.

"You speak of the witch Torie Bliss, do you not?" said the elders.

"Yes. She has lost her powers and we would like you to return them."

"She did not lose her gifts," came the reply.

Just then, lost in the moment, having formless, faceless spirits talk about her as if she were not among them, angered Torie. She forgot herself and found her own voice.

"I have lost them," she said, projecting the words as loudly as she could without the aid of a voice. "I assure you, my friends and I have tried everything; to no avail."

"Torie, no!" said Opal, yanking at the binding that held them together in hopes it would remind Torie of the rules she had agreed to.

"Let her speak," said the elders. "If you are here on her behalf, then she should have a say, don't you think?"

Torie felt the touch of Opal's mind relax a bit as she drifted forward to face the figures sitting in their chairs.

"We know you," said the elders.

If she had possessed skin, Torie would have felt it crawl at that moment.

"What? How do you know me?"

"You are all our children," they said. "Recipients of our hexes at birth. We know you through the untold number of generations through which your magic has flowed. We have felt the touch of your power as it has dispatched those that would do our kind harm. We know you through the touch of your mother as well."

Grief, sadness and apprehension washed over Torie at the mention of her mother.

"My mother? Is…is she here? Is she with you?"

"Only a part of her. The part that joined with us at the moment of her untimely death. We await the full joining of her spirit when it is time."

The full joining? What did that mean?

"Are you saying she isn't here? In the astral plane with you?" Torie asked.

"You know that she is not. She is…elsewhere."

Torie felt a hundred questions bubble within her mind, but before she could ask any of them, she felt the elders pushing at her, driving her slowly back.

"But your mother is not the topic you are here to discuss, is it?" they wailed.

Torie felt the sting of Jasmin's mind lash at her. *Stay on task.*

Again, she steadied her mind and asked the question that had burned for the past few weeks.

"Will I ever wield magic again?"

The elders paused and she could feel a ripple of silent

communication move through them as they considered her request.

"We will not return your magic to you, Torie Bliss."

The silence stung her like a blast of ice-cold water to the face after being out in the sun for too long. That was it. The finality of their tone told her there was no need for further discussion. She had been prepared to beg if it came down to it; at least this way she was spared that indignity.

"Why not?" This time it was Jasmin. She spoke out of turn, allowing her anger to show through her words. Opal moved to silence her, and Torie could feel her friend shrug her off. "No, I want to know why they won't help her. This woman has used her magic for nothing but the betterment of our kind. She has saved lives, both supernatural and human. She is a good person. And I want to know why you won't help her."

Torie felt the elders rise, the space around them thickening. Somewhere in the distance, she thought she heard thunder. She felt the cord that bound them tremble in response to the ire of the elders.

"You dare question us?" they replied. "We do not explain ourselves to anyone or anything, child, but we will tell you this much. The witch known as Torie Bliss does not deserve to have her magic returned to her. She gave it away willingly...we will not return something she obviously did not want."

"No, that isn't true!" Torie yelled into the void. "I did it to save an innocent. And I'd do it again if I had to!"

"Insolent little pup," said the elders. "I suggest you take your leave of us before we decide that none of you are worthy of our gifts."

"Why you—" started Jasmin, but that was all she got out as Opal tugged fiercely at the silver thread.

"And that's enough out of the two of you. Time to go."

And just like that, with the same snap that carried them into the astral world, the three of them were hurled back to their bodies.

Orientation returned slowly to Torie. Her senses were slow to kick back in, and for a moment she thought part of her was still on the astral plane when she opened her eyes and took in the chaos around her.

Everything around them was in disarray. No, that was putting it mildly. Her home had been destroyed...everything was smashed and broken beyond repair. The walls were charred with smoke, the elaborate wainscoting had been blasted to splinters in places, and entire chunks of flooring had been ripped away. There was a hole in the wall where her picture window had once been.

A scream from what had once been her kitchen drew her attention. She jumped to her feet, following closely behind Jasmin as they entered the room. There, in the center of the floor, sat Fionna, holding the body of her wife as she rocked her back and forth.

There was a shuffling of wood, accompanied by a moan that came from Torie's left. There, sticking out from under a mass of wood and granite that had once been her center island, was the lower body of a large, dark-colored wolf.

It was Elric, and he wasn't moving.

Chapter Twelve

"Oh my God," exclaimed Jasmin, rushing to Fionna's side. "What happened?"

The squirrel shifter was too distraught to speak. The only sound that escaped her lips was a heart-wrenching cry that seemed to come from the depths of her very soul. Her voice was raw and hoarse, and she flinched when Jasmin placed a hand on her shoulder. She looked up at the witch through bloodshot eyes, one of which was swollen and black. Her lip was cut and there was a bruise on her cheek as well as a cut across her forehead.

"Fionna! Who did this to you?" Jasmin repeated.

"It was Max. He and the hunter attacked us while you guys were...whatever you were doing."

Jasmin looked around at the devastation. The house was unrecognizable. The once beautiful home now moaned and creaked under pressure. Large parts of the support walls had been knocked out and Jasmin feared the entire home might come crashing down on them at any moment.

"We fought back as much as possible. Honestly, if it

hadn't been for Elric, we would probably be dead. I've never seen a shifter fight like that before; he was incredible, but he couldn't stop them both."

"Why would Max attack like that?" asked Jasmin. She motioned for her sister to help Fionna and Glen while she rushed to Torie's side. "We need to get him out of here. No telling how long this place is going to remain standing."

"Max wasn't himself," said Fionna. "He was working with the hunter. She must have done something to him."

Opal knelt next to Fionna and placed a hand on Glen's forehead. She closed her eyes and hummed, her deep tone reverberating throughout the broken house.

"What are you doing?" asked Fionna.

"Finding her spirit and asking it not to leave her body just yet. She is alive, and I can help her stay that way, but we need to get out of here."

Fionna nodded and stood, holding her wife in both arms as she carried her carefully across the rubble and towards the front door, with Opal close behind her.

"Come on, you two," Opal said, making her way out of the house. "Move it!"

Torie looked up at Jasmin, tears in her eyes. "I won't leave him."

"You won't have to," Jasmin replied. She extended her arms, holding them over the wood and granite that covered Elric. The debris began to glow blue and then floated upward, enough that Torie was able to drag the wolf free. Once he was out of harm's way, Jasmin let the mass drop with a thud. Together they dragged Elric across the floor and towards the front door.

Just as they exited the home, a loud crash erupted, followed by another even louder.

"I don't know what that was but looks like we won't be going back in there," said Jasmin.

They made their way to the driveway and the front lawn where Fionna had laid Glen, resting her gently on her back. Torie and Jasmin dragged Elric over and placed him beside her. His wolf form was nearly as long as Glen, and while his breathing indicated he was not as hurt as she was, he still had not regained consciousness enough to shift back to human.

Opal was focused on Glen, her magic reaching deep into the woman and probing her injuries. Her eyes were closed, and she hummed loudly as her hands moved across the lithe figure before her.

"Here," she said, her hands hovering above the left side of Glen's abdomen. "She's bleeding here."

"Should I call 9-1-1?" asked Fionna.

"Yes, definitely," replied Opal. "I am going to try and stop the bleeding, but she will definitely need medical attention." She dropped her hands and placed two fingers on Glen's neck. "Her pulse is thready." She gently placed her thumb and forefinger on the woman's chin and tilted her head from one side to the other. Like Fionna, her face was bruised and there was a thin line of red seeping from one ear.

Opal sat cross-legged and clasped her hands together before her. She reached out again, holding her hands over Glen's broken body, as she began to chant.

"Most powerful spirit, protector of all,
it is to your power, I now call.
Heal this child's body, cease her pain,
this I ask, in your divine name."

Fionna watched as ghostly green roots made their way up from the ground where Glen lay and covered her body before sinking into the injured woman and becoming part of her.

"Hey—" started Fionna, reaching for her lover.

"It's okay," said Opal, waving for her not to move. "Those are earth spirits. They preserve life. They will help stabilize her until modern medicine can do more." She smiled wearily at Fionna and placed a hand on her arm. "It's alright. She's going to live. I promise."

"Don't suppose you have some extra earth spirits for Elric?" asked Torie. She had watched what had transpired in awe, but now her attention was back on her lover.

Opal moved to sit next to Elric, holding her hands above his body as she hummed.

"He does not need my help. His body is already healing," said Opal. "Shifters are incredibly resilient. Especially werewolves. I've seen them lose a limb and regrow one."

She stopped speaking when she saw the look on Torie's face.

"Good job, Opal," said Jasmin, "all these years and you still haven't learned to read the room."

Opal scowled at her sister but decided against the smart-ass reply that was on the tip of her tongue. Instead, she turned her attention back to Elric.

"His bones aren't broken, so that's good."

"Why is that good?" questioned Torie. "I mean, don't get me wrong, I'm glad, but why is that a good thing?"

"Because he's unconscious," replied Opal. "He can't shift back to his human form. His bones would heal in his wolf shape and then...well, we'd probably have to break them again when he shifted to human form, so they could heal properly. I've seen it done before...it's not pretty."

Torie shuddered inwardly. The thought of causing him more pain than he had already gone through was more than she could bear. Her thoughts were broken by the wail of an ambulance's siren as it made its way up the mountainside.

Minutes later, the side of the house was lit up by flashing lights as the paramedics arrived.

"She has a ruptured spleen," Opal told the young woman who was assisting in getting Glen onto the stretcher. "Liver laceration and ruptured ear drum as well. You need to get her to surgery right away."

The paramedic didn't question her as they loaded her into the back of the ambulance.

"What happened to her?" asked an older man who had been taking notes on a small electronic tablet.

"Gas explosion," said Jasmin, stepping forward. "We were lucky to get out. She was caught in the blast." She saw the man's eyes track to the large wolf lying on the ground. "And so was the family dog."

"Um, okay. Is everyone else okay…do you need a second unit?"

"No. We are fine. Please, can you just get our friend to the hospital as soon as possible?" said Torie.

The driver hesitated only briefly before nodding to the young female to close the doors.

"Wait, I'm going too," said Fionna.

"Are you family?" asked the driver.

The flash of yellow that crossed through Fionna's eyes was nearly enough to make him wet himself as he held the doors open long enough for her to leap inside. He nodded to Torie before climbing behind the wheel and peeling out of her gravel driveway.

"We needed Fionna to tell us more about what happened," said Torie, wrapping her arms around herself.

"No, we don't," said Jasmin. She was looking at Elric, who, for all intents and purposes, appeared to be sleeping. "Whatever happened is locked in his mind. I can get at that."

"Do we need to be worried about cops showing up?" asked Opal. "I mean, I'm surprised they haven't responded already."

"Max has been building the force up out of supernaturals; mainly shifters. They will wait for his orders before they act."

Opal nodded. "That could be bad. If they follow him blindly, and he's under the control of a hunter…" She didn't have to finish that sentence. They all knew what that could mean.

"How can you show us what happened?" asked Torie.

Jasmin smiled. "Magic, of course."

She knelt next to Elric and placed one hand on his head. Eyes closed, she concentrated, pouring her will into his mind, and forcing him to show them what he had seen. She held her other hand out, casting a cloud of mystic power on which the werewolf's memories were projected.

The three of them watched as he was racing through the woods, the foliage being eaten up in increasingly larger leaps as he ran through the forest at dizzying speeds. Ahead of him was Torie's house, and they could see the front door had been blown inward by a kick powerful enough that it took out the frame of the large door.

They felt like they were part of the action as he leapt through the opening just in time to see the hunter draw her knife and aim the point of it at the three witches sitting on the couch, oblivious to everything happening around them.

There was a blast that sounded like thunder to his enhanced hearing, and he watched as the hunter somersaulted backwards, narrowly evading Glen's shotgun. There was a distinctive *shkking* sound as she chambered another round and aimed it at the hunter. At the same time, Fionna leapt at the hunter, leveling a kick at her midsection. The squirrel shifter grunted when the kick landed. To Elric, it sounded like she had kicked a concrete wall.

The hunter actually laughed as she shrugged off the blow, landing an open-handed slap that sent Fionna spiraling through the air away from her.

Then, dodging yet another shot from Glen, the hunter sprinted across the space to confront her. To her credit, rather than try to squeeze off another shot, Glen turned the gun around and landed a blow on the hunter's chin with the butt of the shotgun.

The hunter barely registered the hit. She smiled, rubbing at the spot on her chin where Glen had made contact. Then, she drove her fist into Glen's midsection, sending her flying backwards into the wall that separated the living room from the kitchen. Fionna was on the hunter before she could move to finish Glen off. She shifted in and out of her squirrel form, using the change in size and speed to keep the hunter off balance as she landed blow after blow.

Elric rushed forward, shifting to his half-human hybrid form, only to be caught by something from behind. Something monstrously strong and large. He howled in pain as fangs clamped down on his shoulder and upper chest. He was thrown against the brick fireplace, smashing the stone and sending shards of rock and wood flying.

It was Max, in his full wolf form, yellow eyes blazing as he stared at his fallen beta. The hunter smiled as she landed an open-handed slap on Fionna that sent her spiraling through the wall that Glen had crashed against. Then she strode over to stand next to the great wolf and began to casually stroke his fur.

She cocked her head to one side, smiling at Elric, and uttered a single word.

"Kill."

Immediately, Max launched himself, his razor-sharp fangs aimed at Elric's throat. Elric was able to get up a forearm to protect himself just in time. He screamed as Max's jaws closed on his arm. With his free hand he punched the wolf, aiming for his more sensitive nose, and was rewarded as Max released him, shaking his head. Elric dropped to the floor in front of his friend, drawing both legs up to his chest, he kicked out with all his strength, sending the wolf flying through the air to land on the kitchen island, smashing it to pieces.

He saw the hunter once again draw her knife as she stood over the three witches that were still not moving.

"No!" he screamed, leaping for the hunter.

Fast as he was, she was faster still. She caught him mid leap, one hand clasped firmly about his throat as she held him aloft. He struggled against her grip, but to no avail.

"Bad dog," she said. Tossing him upward to crash into the ceiling, shaking the entire house to its foundation. As Elric's body fell back towards the floor, the hunter spun, landing a vicious side kick to his side that sent him sprawling across the kitchen floor.

Grayness swam in his peripheral vision as he watched the hunter bend forward, leaning over the witches. He tried to stand, but his legs weren't working, and he could feel consciousness slipping away. The last thing he saw was the hunter take something from her pocket and slip it into Jasmin's front jacket pocket.

Then everything went black, and the visions being projected for Torie, Jasmin and Opal stopped.

"What the hell?" said Torie. "Why would she attack like that?"

"More importantly, why didn't she kill us when she had the chance?" asked Opal. She turned to her sister. "And what did she put in your pocket?"

She and Torie crowded around Jasmin, watching as she fished into her jacket. She frowned as she withdrew a small, gold object. She held it in her hand and turned it over, looking closely at it.

"What is that?" Torie asked. "It looks like a locket."

Jasmin didn't speak as she turned it over in her hand. It *was* a locket, intricately detailed with tiny swirls and stars embossed on the cover. Her hands were shaking as she pried it open. The picture inside made her gasp, and she dropped the locket to the ground, her hands flying to her mouth.

Opal bent down and retrieved it, examining the picture as Torie peered over her shoulder.

"Is that…is that you?" asked Opal.

The picture on the locket was of a young woman with delicate features and full, natural hair that was pulled to either side of her head in beautiful afro puffs.

"Jasmin," said Torie, "how does this hunter have a picture of you from so long ago?"

"Because," she replied, her voice trembling, "that hunter is my daughter."

Chapter Thirteen

"I'm sorry, your what?" said an incredulous Torie.

Jasmin hadn't taken her eyes off the locket. "You heard what I said."

"I knew it!" exclaimed Opal, storming over to her sister. "I knew you were hiding something from me. All those years ago when you stopped answering my letters. You cut me out of your life, and I knew it had to be for something other than just what happened with Mom."

Jasmin sat down heavily on the ground. She didn't trust her legs to support her weight. The air around her was growing heavy and she felt herself beginning to gasp for breath.

"Hey, hey, it's going to be okay," said Torie, rushing to her friend's side. She rubbed Jasmin's back as she spoke softly to her. "Breathe…one breath at a time. Slow down… you're okay."

Jasmin audibly exhaled a couple of times before turning to Torie and her sister.

"Am I? Going to be okay?" Tears streamed down her

face. "I can't believe this is happening. After all these years of forcing myself to bury her and not think about her. Now, here she is, face to face with me."

"Well, I guess that explains why she didn't just kill us," said Opal.

Torie gave her a stern look. "Jasmin, I don't even know what to say."

"I do," said Opal, "how about, why didn't you tell anyone you had a daughter? Are you even sure she *is* your daughter?"

Jasmin nodded, turning the locket over and over in her hand before holding it up by the chain.

"This is the only thing I left her with," she said. "When I—" her voice faltered and she buried her face in her hands, letting her tears flow.

Torie sat beside her and threw an arm around her, drawing her in close. "Shhh, it's okay. We can talk about this later." She rocked her, letting Jasmin cry for what felt like hours.

Opal sat down beside her as well. She fished around in her bag and found a white handkerchief.

"It's clean," she said, offering it up. "I'm sorry for what I just said. I really need to learn to edit the things that come out of my mouth before I just spew them out. I can't imagine what you went through that led you to make whatever decisions you had to make."

Torie nodded. "If you need to tell us anything, you know you can. I'm not here to judge you; Lord knows I'm the last person who should be passing judgement. I'm here for you, and I support whatever you need."

Jasmin took the white cloth and pressed it to her face, drying her eyes and cheeks.

"It was just after you left," she said, turning to Opal.

She took her sister's hand and gave it a squeeze. "Gram had passed, and I just felt so alone. And tired. Tired in a way that I didn't think was possible. The guilt I felt over Mom was more than I could bear. Couple with that the fact that I blamed myself for you leaving, and I was in a very dark place."

Opal looked like she had just taken a shot to the stomach. Jasmin took her hand in both of hers.

"No, I'm not trying to make you feel guilty. All of this was generated in my head and I didn't know what to do. I completely understand why you left...at least now I do. I was just looking for someone to blame for the space I was in and since there was no one else around..." She shrugged, squeezing Opal's hand. "What I'm saying is that I created the cage that I felt trapped in; no one else had a hand in that."

"Still, if I had been there, things might have turned out differently."

"Maybe. Or I could have found other destructive vices to fall into. But I felt alone and was looking for something... some*one*...to help make me feel better." She took a deep breath before continuing. "I did the usual; drinking, sampling a few mind-altering substances here and there. And men of course. But none of those did anything for me other than providing a temporary haze to get lost in. It was like using a band aid to cover a gunshot wound; did nothing to staunch the emotional bleeding I was suffering.

"So one evening, feeling particularly down, the little bit of money I had from the sale of Gram's house was drying up, and I didn't have a clue what I needed to do to get out of the mess I was in. I went to a party out at the lake; the parties Mom had always told us we weren't allowed to go to."

Opal nodded. "I remember. The ones filled with all the low life townies, as Mom used to call them. She said if we hung out with them, we'd end up just like them; no futures."

"That's right," said Jasmin. "Well, guess what? Mom was right. One of those low lifes was a man I caught myself dating. Truth is, we were just using each other for what we could offer at the time, but that seemed to be what I needed in that moment. But something was different that night. I was tired of the partying. Tired of feeling like I was walking around in a daze. I felt on edge watching everyone get wasted around me. I needed a change and told Kenny, the low life, that this wasn't working for me any longer and I needed to make a change in my life. I was leaving, and he knew that it wasn't just for the night.

"What I didn't tell him, was that I had just found out I was pregnant. That was why I wasn't drinking that night. For the first time in so long I had a clear head and realized that this was a life I had condemned myself to, but it didn't have to be one my child would be locked into."

She paused, exhaling sharply. Torie felt her body lighten, as if the weight of the world had been lifted from her shoulders.

"Not a day has gone by that I haven't thought about her and wondered what happened to her," she said.

"Can we ask what happened with her?" said Torie.

They waited as Jasmin gathered herself, choosing her words carefully.

"I'm not proud of what I did next. I knew that I couldn't care for a child. Hell, I wasn't even able to take care of myself. And I knew; I just knew, deep down in my bones that I was carrying a little girl. I just knew. And that scared me more than anything. That I was bringing another girl, another potential witch, into this world to follow in my failed footsteps."

"So you gave her up for adoption?" said Opal.

Jasmin didn't answer. She stared into the distance, letting the silence between them build.

"No, I didn't," she said finally, her voice little more than a whisper. "I left her outside of a fire station." Here she burst into tears, too ashamed to look her friends in the eyes.

Thunder rolled in the distance, and Opal's eyes grew pale as her power built.

"You did what?" demanded the witch. Blue lightning streaked across the sky in the distance. The pulse of light playing through the growing clouds was echoed in Opal's pale eyes. She stood, thunder echoing all around her. "Tell me you didn't do that, Jasmin."

"What was I supposed to do, Opal?" she replied. "What choices did I have? I couldn't bring myself to abort. I looked into adoption, but it's not like people would have been knocking down the door to raise the child of a poor, black girl from the coal mining mountains! What were my options? I was alone!"

The thunder rumbled in the distance but faded as Opal reeled her power in. She glanced at Torie whose eyes were wide with empathy.

"Stop this," Torie said, directing her attention to Opal. "We don't know what Jasmin was thinking, what decisions she had to be grappling with. This had to be the hardest decision she has ever had to make."

Opal settled down and turned to her sister.

"You went through so much by yourself, Jasmin. But this...why didn't you reach out to me? I would have been there for you. You had to have known that."

"I didn't know anything. All I knew was that I couldn't

raise a child. I had nothing to offer her. I felt like nothing myself; I was broken. I did what I thought I had to at the time."

"What about the father?" said Torie. "Does he know?"

Jasmin exhaled. "I tried that. I told him I was pregnant. I guess part of me wanted to hold onto the hope that maybe, just maybe, he'd want to help. That he'd want to make us a family. But I was a fool to think that. Rather than sympathy or love, I was met with rage from him. He said that it probably wasn't his, that it could belong to any number of men in the town. I told him that wasn't true, and that I had only been with him. Anger made my tongue sharp that night. I told him that unlike him, I was a loyal lover. I wasn't lying down with anyone that could offer a full bottle of gin or a fresh hit of weed. That earned me a split lip. So I knew he would be no help. He offered to pay for me to end the pregnancy. I took him up on it...took his money and left. That was the last I saw of him."

Torie felt her anger spill down her cheeks in the form of fresh tears. How could any man be so callous? The answer to that was obvious; it wasn't a man that Jasmin had been dealing with. No man would act that way, but she would never say that to her friend.

"So did you think about it?" said Opal. "Ending the pregnancy, I mean."

Jasmin didn't say anything at first, but then she let out a little sigh. "I'd be lying if I said I didn't. But in the end, I knew that was not an option. My actions brought a life into this world; but I'd be damned if I'd let them take one out as well. So when the time came, I—and I'm not proud of this —I left her at a fire department."

Torie could see the anger and judgement in Opal's eyes,

and she waved the woman off before she could voice her opinion.

"I mean, I stayed close by where I could see that someone came out and picked her up. I didn't just drop her and run. I left her with a note and the gold locket that Mom had given me when I was a baby." She looked at Opal. "You remember, you got one too."

Opal stared at her sister before shrugging. "I don't remember that."

"Well, you had one. We didn't wear them however, we kept them in a small antique jewelry box in the bedroom we shared."

Something in Opal's eyes told them a memory had been sparked. Still, she didn't acknowledge anything, rather she just stared at her sister, urging her to go on.

"If you're wondering why I didn't take her to a hospital, the answer is I was afraid. Afraid they would ask me questions or call the police. I couldn't risk that."

"Did you…think about keeping her?" asked Torie.

"No. In all honesty I knew I couldn't raise a child. What kind of life could I have offered?"

"Did you think about the fact that she would grow into her powers without anyone there to guide her?" questioned Opal, trying hard to control her tone.

"That was just it," I said. "I thought that maybe, if she grew up without the influence of magic all around her, maybe it wouldn't happen to her and she'd just be normal."

"Normal?" said Opal. "Do you think there is something wrong with us, Jasmin?"

"No, that isn't what I meant. Opal, we had no one to guide us. We knew what Gram could do, but that was it. It's one thing to be told you're going to grow up and get all these magical abilities, but until it happens, it seems so nebulous and far-fetched. I had no idea how wonderful our powers would turn out to be. For all I knew, it might not have happened at all."

"Well, I can tell you that even with an absent mother, it still happens," said Torie.

"I know that now. But when I was a child...I was ignorant. That's all I can say on the matter."

They sat in silence for a while. Torie went to check on Elric, leaving the two sisters to talk. She could feel the silence between them and knew that conversation was a ways off still. Instead, Opal made her way over to the wounded werewolf and held her hands over his chest, head cocked to one side as if she were listening for something.

"He's strong. Nearly completely healed. He should be waking up any minute now." She stood up and made her way back to her sister. "Meanwhile, time to check in on something."

She stretched her hand out and snapped her finger. "To me, my pet."

Immediately, a black, ghostly figure comprised only of smoke glided upward from the ground. It was formless as it settled next to her.

"The hell is that?" asked Jasmin, stepping back.

"My familiar, of course," said Opal. "You do know what a familiar is, right?"

Jasmin looked at her, blinking. "Of course I do. But aren't they usually cats, or some other small house animal?"

"Don't be ridiculous. A familiar can be any sentient being. Granted, most are animals, but in some cases...they can be other." She waved her hand in the direction of the smoke form standing near her. In response, it lengthened its form and wrapped itself around her playfully. "Wait, do you have familiars?"

"No," said Torie, joining the conversation, her eyes glued to the amorphous smoke creature.

"Well, mine never leaves my side. He may not always be seen, but he's always close by. Unless I send him on a mission, as I did earlier. Now tell me, my pet, what have you found?"

The creature hovered next to Opal, audibly whispering to her. The familiar's voice sounded like the wind sighing across a meadow to Torie as she tried in vain to make out what was being said.

Opal turned her head and stared hard at Torie, her eyebrows arched.

"What? What is it?" demanded Jasmin.

"He says that the people in town are using magic. Magic that smells like...you, Torie."

"What? That can't be."

"Oh, it is," said Elric, his voice low and strained as he struggled to sit up.

"Easy there, lay back. I have you," said Torie, rushing to his side and placing an arm around him.

"I'll be okay," he said. "But your smoke monster, or whatever it is, is correct. The humans in town are playing around with magic. Your magic."

Chapter Fourteen

The fireplace crackled, spreading warmth throughout the first floor of Jasmin's house as she set about making a large pot of coffee, while Torie started warming leftover lasagne she had found in the refrigerator. She had already cooked an entire pound of bacon and sat it before a starving Elric, who was devouring it unashamedly.

"Someone forgot to eat," said Jasmin, playfully.

Elric looked up sheepishly from the plate of meat.

"It's okay," she said, "I was just teasing you. I know you need the protein to help heal. Eat up." She turned her attention to Opal as she entered the kitchen. "So, where's your familiar?"

"Oh, he's around. You might not be able to see him, but he doesn't stray far from my side unless I instruct him to."

"So tell us more about what he was able to find out," said Torie. She had not been able to focus on much since they left her destroyed house. What the familiar told Opal, combined with what Elric had said, had consumed her thoughts on the ride back to Jasmin's home.

"Yes," echoed Jasmin. "Maybe that will give us a clue as to not only what has been going on in town lately, but it may offer some insight into what the…hunter is doing here in Singing Falls."

The group caught her hesitation before she said the word hunter, but no one said anything.

"Unfortunately, there isn't a lot to tell," said Opal. "Your townsfolk, the non-supernatural ones, have stumbled onto a source of magic and are experimenting with it. Metrian, my familiar, said they were not doing anything mischievous with it; some were enchanting their vacuums to clean automatically, levitating small objects, things like that. All in the comfort of their own homes, so it doesn't sound like anyone has taken their newfound skills to the public. Yet.

"As for the hunter, your guess is as good as mine. I thought you said she was here to kill the wolves?"

"But she didn't do that," said Jasmin. "And she had every chance." She glanced at Elric.

The wolf nodded. "Jasmin's right. She could have killed us. Instead, she has Max under her control and was using him to attack his friends."

"And how did she do that?" asked Torie. "I thought hunters were fighters, not witches."

"Most hunters are," said Opal. "But this particular hunter has magic in her veins." She gave her sister a look before continuing. "That's something no one has seen before."

"But it's magic that she can't take advantage of," said Torie. "She's not of age."

Opal nodded. "True. Under normal circumstances I would agree. But thanks to you, there are pockets of wild magic out there. Magic that she may be able to tap into easier than most."

"Wild magic?" said Jasmin. "What is that?"

"I've heard of it, but never come across it," said Opal. "All of our hex magic comes from the ancients on the astral plane. Sometimes, a tear in the veil between our world and that of the ancients can occur. When that happens, magic can seep through and settle in this world. It isn't anchored to anything, and before you know it, humans and, in some cases animals, can learn to tap into it."

"And you think we have one of those leaks around here?" asked Elric.

"No. I think she is your leak." Opal pointed to Torie. "Not intentionally of course, but when you gave up your powers, they had to go somewhere."

"Of course," said Jasmin. "Our hex magic is a form of energy; it can neither be created nor destroyed."

Opal was nodding. "When you released your magic, it became free-flowing. Now, it's finding a home."

Torie didn't speak. Brow furrowed, she sat down in a chair next to Elric. "So, all of this is truly my fault. Max being taken, all the craziness that is going on in town. The violence around us." Her voice trailed off as she radiated sadness and fear.

"Now *that* I don't know about," said Jasmin. "I mean, both Elric and Opal's familiar said the magic was being used by humans. But so far, the violence in town has been between the supernaturals. And to my knowledge, supernaturals can't use magic, even if they wanted to."

"Why not?" asked Torie.

"Because they are created from magic. You're right," said Opal. She could see the confusion still present on Torie's face. "We can wield magic because we are empty at birth. The magic in humans is something that rushes in to fill that space when the time comes. But shifters, vampires, elves…they are born with their own kind of magic; the kind that lets them exist. There is no room for a second type of magic to exist within. It's just not possible."

"Then what's causing them to turn on each other like we've seen?" asked Torie.

"I don't know," said Jasmin. "But there has to be a connection. You giving up your powers, everything going screwy in town, and now a hunter showing up that has somehow been able to bring Max under her control." She shook her head. "It can't be a coincidence."

Torie and Opal exchanged glances. A look that didn't escape Jasmin's notice.

"What? What is it?"

"Jasmin, are you sure this is something you want to get involved in?" asked Torie. "I mean, you're incredibly close to all of this, and maybe you should—"

"I should what? Sit this one out? Why? Because the daughter I gave up more than a couple of decades ago has come back to haunt me? And by haunt, I mean kill."

Torie looked her friend in the eye warmly. "Yes. To all of that. And we don't know what that hunter has planned. No one is saying she wants to kill you."

"No but she wants to kill *us*, me and Max," said Elric. "I'm betting she hasn't killed him yet because she needs both our hides to collect her bounty. She's using Max to bring me out."

"Then why didn't she do it back at the house?" questioned Torie. "She could have easily killed you. For that matter, she had us all dead to rights. But she didn't do it. Why?"

No one spoke as they all contemplated Elric's words.

"I have another question. If we all come from a line of witches, why was your daughter born a hunter? Assuming they are born that way, I mean. Or is there some hunter training school out there that she stumbled upon?" asked Torie.

"Good question," said Opal. "Think of it like this; hunters came into being to balance the paranormal scales. They ensure balance in the supernatural world. They keep certain elements in check. Think of what it would be like if there were only deer and antelope in the world, and no wolves and lions. Or, more precisely, there were only lions and wolves. Nothing to prevent them from doing what apex predators are inclined to do. No offense." She nodded in Elric's direction.

"None taken," he replied. "You are right. The hunters are the boogeyman to supernaturals. But I must confess, until now, I wasn't sure they really existed. Humans who had the strength and prowess to hunt even the mightiest among us. You can imagine why I would think them fables."

Torie nodded slowly. "I could see that. But that doesn't answer my question. Are they born or created?"

"Perhaps a little of both. They are born with something that gives them an edge over the rest of humanity; strength, agility, speed, senses. But they have to be trained. Taught how to use those powers to hunt supernatural beings. They have a mentor who finds them at a certain point in their childhood and takes them from their parents. That mentor then teaches them the ways of the hunters. They also teach them the code of the hunters as well," said Opal.

"Code? What kind of code?" asked Torie.

"That you don't work as a bounty hunter. Your skills are sacred, and the duty of a hunter is to serve mankind. Not their own base needs," said Jasmin. She had moved over next to one of the large windows that framed her backyard and was staring out.

"Well, your daughter must have skipped hunter training-school that day," mumbled Opal. She saw the steely look Torie gave her and shrugged. "All I'm saying is that something is off with this particular hunter. If she's working for a mob boss who is using her to extract vengeance, then she has broken the hunter's code."

"So is the power they are born with magical in nature?" asked Torie. "If so, wouldn't that mean she can't wield magic either?"

"Wielding and possessing are not the same thing," said Opal. "She has objects of divinity on her. Those are objects that have been charged with magic of some kind. That rope she wields, for instance, definitely a divinity object. I'm betting that's how she got control of Max; she slipped one on him that allows her to exert influence."

"Elric, why didn't you and Max stay together?" asked Torie.

"Because he was convinced we could cover more ground apart than together. Which is true, but neither of us considered we might run into that hunter. When Fionna and Glen got the call to come back here, we figured we'd take one last sweep through town and call it a night. We split up and I headed into town while he checked some of the areas that lay to the west, near the lake.

"I was passing through town when a woman walked past me, and I caught her scent. It was the same one from the bakery. The one at the table you pointed out. I noticed that there was a man with her. A man with no scent at all."

"Just like at the bakery," said Torie, excitedly. "When the table was obviously set for two, but you said your senses only registered one person sitting there! Same as at the bar where the fight broke out."

Elric was nodding. "Exactly. I heard the man call her by name; Myra."

"The same woman that Glen recognized as having the dead husband," said Jasmin.

"Yep. And get this, she referred to him as 'husband' while they were talking as well."

"But Glen said she saw her husband die," added Jasmin.

"That's why I decided to follow them. Something didn't feel right with them. There was nothing tangible about this man at all; if I closed my eyes, it was like he disappeared from the world."

"Where did they go?" asked Torie.

"I followed them back to what I assume was their home. Once they disappeared inside, I crept as close as possible to listen to what was going on. They were in the basement, and I managed to find a small window around back that I could peep through. I couldn't make out what they were doing, but I could hear them. The man was crying. He was asking the woman why something wasn't working. She was assuring him everything could be fixed, and that it just took time. Then, he cried more, and she comforted him. But that was it. Before I could make out anything else, Max called. He said he could see the hunter taking a path that led directly to your house. He told me to get there as soon as possible."

"We need to figure out how she is controlling Max," said Torie. "If she can do that to him, then she can do it to Elric as well."

"And that means you're all but useless to us in a fight," said Jasmin. "She has one wolf at her side; we can't risk her getting her hands on another. If she hasn't killed Max yet, then something tells me she's waiting on you; a matching set."

"So where does that leave us?" asked Opal. "Guess it's down to just you and me, sis."

Torie stepped forward. "No, there are three of us."

Opal smiled. "No offense, Torie, but you're down for the count. At this point you're more a liability than the wolf."

Torie tried to ignore the sting of Opal's words, even though she knew they were true. Still, she wasn't quite ready to lie down and roll over. A couple of days ago, maybe; but not now.

"Yeah, you can stop right there with all of that," replied Torie. "I'm not sitting anything out. Now, it just so happens that I agree with you about Elric. But if you think I'm going to go crawl into a hole somewhere and hide while you solve a problem that I might have caused, you're crazy. And let's not forget that it was my house that was just destroyed. Wherever you're going, I'm going."

"And where she goes, I go," said Elric.

Torie started to argue but saw the look on his face and knew it would be pointless. Instead, she just smiled and gave him a nod.

"Well, aren't we just the bunch?" said Opal. "A witch with no powers, a wolf that's susceptible to a hunter's control, and a woman with a super-strong, homicidal daughter that she gave up at birth. All stuck in a town with a bunch of humans playing with magic they don't understand. Where do we start?"

Torie laughed. "Oh, please. That's easy. We start with the only lead we have. Namely, Myra Simms' house and her maybe-not-so-dead husband."

"And the hunter?" Opal asked, giving Jasmin a quick look.

"One thing at a time," said Torie. "For all we know this could be tied in with the hunter. We look into this first, then find a way to break Max free of the hunter. Then, we decide what to do about...her." She didn't want to look at her friend. Jasmin's pain was palpable and the thought of a mother having to square off against her own daughter was more than Torie wanted to think about at the moment.

Whatever came next, she knew she would stand by her friend. She just hoped that any of them would be able to do what had to be done if it came down to making sure their friends, and their town, were safe.

Chapter Fifteen

Even though they protested, Torie made certain that everyone ate something before piling into the car to drive back into town. Jim's Bakery was still closed without a reopening date in sight, so that meant there would be no option for bagels or muffins if someone were to get hungry before returning to town.

"And by someone I'm assuming you mean me," Jasmin had said, pointedly.

"If the hangry-pains fit…" said Torie.

"What's hangry?" asked Opal.

"It's what happens to your sister when she gets angry and hungry at the same time. It's not pretty."

Other than Elric, that drew a chuckle from all of them. Torie knew what he was feeling. The thought of someone you cared about being in mortal danger was enough to make you sick; and it drove all other thoughts from your mind. She smiled at him, will strength and support to her lover.

Elric rode in the front, giving directions to Jasmin, while

Torie and Opal sat silently in the back seat. Torie looked around, briefly wondering if Opal's familiar was in the car with them, or how that worked. She was about to ask, but then thought better of it, preferring to sit and contemplate the things that were better suited to her understanding.

Like what they would do if they ran into the hunter again. She looked at the back of Jasmin's head, worried about her friend. As if she could sense what was happening, Jasmin lifted her eyes momentarily to the rearview mirror and gave Torie a hard look, accompanied by a nod.

Whatever needed doing, she would be up for the task. At least that's what her eyes said.

After twenty minutes of silent driving, other than Elric giving the random turn left or right commands, they pulled into the driveway of a modest brick ranch home situated on a lovely property lined with large, mature trees and beautifully cropped Crepe Myrtles dotting the front lawn.

Once they walked up to the front door, Elric moved to knock, but Jasmin stopped him.

"Let me," she said. "Whatever else we may be dealing with, Myra Simms is a school teacher. She may not even open the door to a stranger with angry eyes."

"What? I don't have angry eyes. Do I, Torie?"

He turned to his lover only to have her avert her eyes and offer him a slight shrug.

"Maybe just intense," she offered. "But either way, let Jasmin knock."

Torie found herself holding her breath as Jasmin knocked three times on the door. She had no idea who or what would answer, but if she had learned anything over the past few months living in a town of supernaturals, it was to always be ready. With no magic to draw on, she shoved her hand into her pocket, feeling for the small, white gemstone Jasmin had gifted her.

They waited patiently before Jasmin knocked again. She leaned forward, her ear close to the door. "I don't hear anything."

"Let the big bad wolf listen," said Opal. She rolled her eyes at the look Jasmin gave her, but smiled as Elric stepped forward, his head cocked to one side.

"I don't hear anyone at all in the house." He gave the air a sniff. "No scents either. The place is empty."

"Good," said Jasmin. She pointed a finger at the door handle and popped the lock in such a way that the door drifted open. "Oh look, the door's open. Maybe we should go inside to make sure no one broke in."

"What are you doing?" said Torie. "We aren't cops, we can't just go wandering into someone's house."

"Why not?" said Opal. "I mean, the door is open, I feel like I was invited inside."

"It's open because…oh, never mind. Let's just get this over with." Torie pushed past them and entered a small, but comfortably appointed, living room. There was a matching sofa and loveseat, each covered in a vibrant fabric bursting with bright flowers. A spindle-legged chair sat to one side, next to a tall cocktail table with a turquoise blue lamp that was slightly too big for the supporting table. An old, box television, complete with rabbit ears, sat in one corner.

It looked like the room had been frozen in time.

"Elric," said Torie, "how old was this couple?"

The wolf shrugged. "Not sure. I'm not good with guessing human ages; but I'd say she was late sixties, and he was at least a decade older than her."

"What would a teacher at the local school and her

elderly, supposedly dead, husband have to do with outbreaks of violence among shifters in town?" wondered Jasmin.

They briefly walked through the house, checking the tiny kitchen and two back bedrooms. Everything in the house was pristine; from the perfectly arranged bric-a-brac to the dusted shelves and tightly made beds. Nothing was out of place.

"It's almost too clean," said Torie. "This place looks like it's barely been lived in."

"Well, we've looked through every room except the basement. We can give that the once over and see if anything looks amiss there."

"I still feel guilty about rummaging through these people's house," said Torie as they made their way to a closed door that opened to a narrow stairwell. "You're sure this is the same woman whose scent you caught at the bar and bakery?"

Elric nodded. "Absolutely." He paused upon the stairs, lifting his head slightly and sampling the air.

"What is it?" asked Torie, nervously.

"Something…unpleasant," he replied.

Torie felt a chill move up her spine as she saw his claws descend from his fingertips. Whatever he sensed had triggered something in him, and he maneuvered his body on the stairs until he was standing directly in front of her.

"I feel it too," said Jasmin. She held both hands in front of her, each encircled by glowing blue light. "There is something down here."

As one they moved down the steps, Jasmin in front, followed by Elric, Torie and Opal.

"What is that smell?" Torie screwed up her nose.

"I've never smelled anything like it," said Jasmin.

"I have," whispered Opal. "And I pray to God it's not what I think it is."

Torie wanted to ask her to clarify her remark, but the scent in the air had grown considerably as they reached the bottom of the stairs, and when she opened her mouth to speak it clawed at the back of her throat. She found herself struggling for the words to describe it. There was the heavy scent of wet dirt, but it was combined with the coppery smell of fresh blood, something that made her think of a three covered in peat moss, all overlaid on something that smelled sweet but almost rotting.

The stairs descended into a small, cramped space with a low ceiling. Boxes stored against a far wall were illuminated by the glow of Jasmin's magic. Water lines reached halfway up their sides, indicating the space had definitely flooded at some point, and Torie wondered if maybe that was the source of the smell. Water damaged cardboard plus whatever was housed in them.

There was a single, naked light bulb swinging from the ceiling which Elric flicked on by pulling the string attached. The naked glare showed there wasn't much more to the room. There were stacks of folding chairs and a couple of card tables leaning against one wall, along with more boxes marked "Christmas" and "Books".

Low, wooden crossbeams covered in spiderwebs crossed the ceiling, intersecting open pipes and visible wiring. They walked from the main room through an open door into yet another damp space, this one had fluorescent lights strung across the wooden beams that whitewashed the room and the friends in an unflattering glare at the flip of a light switch on the wall. This room was empty except for a series of large, five gallon buckets that sat in the very center of the space.

Whatever was in them emanated the sickening smell, and Torie nearly gagged as they approached the buckets. Jasmin held out her hand, increasing her magical glow as they peered into the containers.

"What the hell is that?" demanded Jasmin.

"It looks like...mud," said Elric. His nose was wrinkled at the stench, and he felt the hair on the back of his neck stand up. "Every instinct I have is telling me to leave this place." His voice was low and gruff, and Torie could tell he was on the verge of shifting into his wolf form in response to whatever it was they were looking at.

His initial assessment seemed pretty accurate to Torie. Holding her breath, she peered closer into one of the buckets. They were all filled with the same brackish, wet-looking substance. For all intents and purposes, it looked like a bucket of black, wet dirt. She reached out a hand only to have it smacked away by Opal.

"Ow," she said.

"Don't go touching stuff you know nothing about," said Opal. "Hasn't my sister taught you anything?"

"You have words," said Torie, shaking out her hand. "You could have used them, you know."

"Opal, do you know what this is?" asked Jasmin.

She nodded. "I do. But what it's doing here, in the home of a human, is the real question."

"Uh, no, the real question is what the hell is it?" said Torie.

"It's called motor-nekros. An ancient word from the hex language, the language of witches, that means *dead water.*"

Jasmin frowned. "Why does that sound familiar...?"

Before Opal could answer, Elric let out a low warning growl. Dropping to the ground, he shifted to his wolf form and slowly advanced to the very back of the room where there appeared to be another small room. The door entering it was tiny and little more than a cut-out in the concrete wall, trimmed with black wood. It was faintly lit by another naked lightbulb, and if Elric had not pointed it out, the witches may not have even noticed it.

"Torie, stay behind us," said Jasmin.

She and Elric approached the room slowly, with Opal staying close to Jasmin. At some point she had summoned her familiar and it floated behind them; an extra set of eyes to keep watch over their backside.

Stepping into the room, they were assaulted by a new smell. One that had been shielded by the overpowering sweetness of the mud in the previous space. This was a smell they all recognized.

The rot of human flesh.

Tori gagged and held her arm up, resting her nose in the crook of her elbow for protection. The glow from Jasmin's magic illuminated the room with the wattage of a hundred lamps.

Like the others, this room was sparse with only a few boxes against one wall. Unlike the rest however, this room was dominated by a large pool table that hulked in the middle of the open space. There was something lying on it; something they could barely make out, even in the glare from Jasmin's light.

They approached it, standing at the edge of the table and looking down. It was a figure, small and diminutive. Not much bigger than a five-year-old. But upon closer inspection they realized it wasn't a child, but rather something that had been molded into the shape of a child. It was formed from the dark mud that was in the previous room, and it lay on the table, black and glistening in the light.

"What the hell?" said Torie. "Why does it smell like something dead?"

"That's not where the smell is coming from," said Jasmin. She nudged her friend, directing her attention to Elric. He was moving slowly towards the back of the room where the only other piece of furniture sat.

It was a bed, covered in threadbare sheets and a plain, tattered blue blanket.

Sitting on the edge of the bed was an old man. His feet were planted on the floor and his spine was ramrod straight. He was perfectly still, eyes as dark as night were focused on the wall in front of him. In his arms he held a body. One that was badly decomposing in his grip.

It was the body of Myra Simms, and her husband sat motionless, cradling her in his stiff arms.

Chapter Sixteen

Elric was sniffing at the man, a low, rumbling growl emanating from him as he inched closer.

"Elric, no," said Opal. "Stay back. Let us handle this. And whatever you do, don't get any mud on you."

Both Torie and Jasmin looked at her questioningly.

"Trust me," she said, glancing their direction before returning her attention to the man sitting on the bed. "Please ask him to stand down." She motioned in Elric's direction.

Torie nodded and motioned for the wolf to return to her side. Only when he was standing beside her did he revert to his human form.

"He's not real," said Elric to Torie and Jasmin. "Whatever that is, it's not a man. It has to be what was with the woman at the bar."

Torie felt the hair on the back of her neck stir as she watched Opal slowly approach him, her hands at her sides, fingers splayed and palms out, indicating that she was not armed and meant no harm.

"Mr. Simms," she said, her tone even and low, "can you hear me?"

There was no reply from the man, or whatever he was. Torie squinted, trying to see if he was breathing. He was as still as a statue, and she wasn't sure he was even alive.

"Mr. Simms, my name is Opal and I'm not here to hurt you. I'm just going to move right here and sit beside you for a moment." She made her way to a spot on the bed next to him and sat down, careful not to disturb the feet of the woman he held that were resting on the blanket next to him.

"What is she doing?" Torie whispered to Jasmin, who responded with a shrug.

Opal continued speaking softly to the man beside her.

"Is that your wife? She looks very tired. I am sure she is grateful to you for holding her all this time, but I'm betting she would be more comfortable lying on the bed. And I'm sure you must be tired as well; it can't be easy sitting there, holding onto her for so long. How long have you been like this? All day? Since yesterday?"

Still there was no response, and the witch looked at her friends before continuing.

"Why don't you let us help you? We can take her and place her on the bed where she can rest; and you can relax and tell us what happened."

She reached slowly for the woman in his arms just as Torie and Jasmin moved to step closer to them.

That was when the man's head snapped around to stare at them, freezing Torie and Jasmin in their tracks. His black, unblinking eyes locked on them. They were flat and emotionless and for some reason Torie found them extremely sad.

Following Opal's lead, she approached the man slowly.

As she got closer, she could make out more of his features. He was elderly, probably in his late seventies, with a shock of unkempt, white hair. Deep lines covered his forehead and around his sagging cheeks. Age spots dotted his face and flowed across his reddish nose. The skin on his face was thin; so much so that she could make out the thin veins that ran across his temples where his thinning hair had retreated.

But it was his eyes that dominated his face. Large, black ovals, with no irises or visible eyelids. They were like small saucers in the middle of his face, and the fact that they were fixed on her made her even more uneasy. Still, she inched forward, keeping her eyes locked on his.

"She's right," she said. "We aren't here to hurt anyone. We just want to help, if you'll let us."

She reached over and tentatively placed a hand on the woman's foot. It was cold and stiff and Torie fought her instinct to recoil from the feel.

This was obviously someone the man cared about greatly. She felt her heart bottom out at the thought of loving someone as much as he surely did to sit there holding their cold flesh for so long.

The man held her gaze but didn't move as she took the woman's feet and slowly swung her legs off his lap. Torie nodded to Opal, who leaned forward and slipped her arm around the woman's torso. Briefly the man stiffened as the weight of the body was lessened. Opal paused long enough for him to relax and then resumed taking the body out of his arms. She stood at the same time as Torie, and together they lifted the woman away from him to place her body on the bed. She was beginning to stiffen, so they lay her on her side in a semi-fetal position.

The man still sat there, just as he had, arms bent and out in front of him as if he still held her body.

Even though he had turned to face her and seemed to be staring right through her, Torie waved her hand in front of his face. He didn't respond to that either. Not sure what her option might be, she reached out and took one of his hands in hers. To her surprise, he squeezed slightly, and did not resist when she gently lowered his arm so that his hand rested in his lap.

"Mr. Simms," said Torie, "can you speak? Can you tell us what happened here?"

When he didn't answer, Jasmin stepped forward and tentatively placed her forefinger on his forehead. Closing her eyes, she whispered an incantation to herself. She remained like that for nearly a minute before stepping back.

"Nothing," she said. "There are no residual memories inside this man. It's like he's...empty. I've never felt anything like it." She looked at Opal and nodded, then stepped back.

Opal placed a hand on the man's head and spoke to him. "Mr. Simms, I'm going to try something. I won't hurt you. I promise."

Then she looked at her familiar and gave a nod.

Without hesitation, the smoke flowed across the floor, reassembling in front of the old man, before slowly entering his body, becoming one with the human its master now held in thrall.

Torie and Jasmin watched closely, not sure what was being done or what to expect. Almost immediately, the old man's body stiffened even more. His torso jerked spasmodically to one side, almost as if he were trying to pull away from Opal's grip. She placed her palm flat on his forehead and gripped his thigh with the other, holding fast.

Torie placed a comforting hand on the man's shoulder, massaging him gently.

142

"It's okay," she intoned, softly.

Then, before anyone could act, the man stood. The suddenness of his movement threw Torie's hand off, and he turned to face her, his previously emotionless face now a mask of rage. He roared, shoving Opal away from him as he rounded on Torie, shoulders squared, fists clenched.

Instantly, Elric was at her side. He had shifted into his hybrid form, and grabbed the man by the arm, a warning growl escaping his wolfen mouth.

The old man moved with surprising speed. Before Elric could react, he grabbed the wolf by his arm and with little discernible effort, threw Elric across the room to crash against the stone wall. Collapsing to the floor, Elric shifted to his full wolf form. Howling in anger, he bared his fangs as he crouched, ready to spring at the man. Opal moved to stand in front of him, holding her arm out to stop his attack,

"Elric, wait," she said. "Let me try something."

Waving an arm, she motioned to the man, or rather to the familiar inside the man. Smoke curled out of the old man's nose, mouth and ears as Opal's familiar left his body, only to coalesce as it re-formed, standing next to the witch.

Immediately the old man calmed, his body losing its rigor; yet he continued to stare at Torie, his black eyes and face once more devoid of feelings.

"What the hell was that?" demanded Jasmin, rushing over to Torie and Opal. "Are you two okay?"

"We're fine," said Torie, answering for both of them. "I don't think he was trying to hurt us; he just lashed out at whatever Opal's familiar did to him."

"I asked my familiar to meld with him, see if maybe it could pick up what our magic could not," said Opal.

"And?" asked Jasmin. She watched as Torie moved to stand beside a now human Elric. "What did it find out?"

Opal's familiar twisted and flowed around her, circling her body like a translucent python. She closed her eyes, letting the images the familiar had gathered flow into her mind. When she opened them, her eyes glowed white in the dimly lit room.

"Just as I thought," she said. "This man is a golem."

Jasmin and Torie just stared at her. Elric's eyes lit up.

"I knew it!" he said.

"Oh, you knew it, huh?" said Opal. "Then why didn't you save us all some time and effort and tell us sooner?" Elric looked away sheepishly. "Yeah, that's what I thought."

"I meant, I didn't know the word for it, but it explains his...emptiness."

"Okay, for the rest of us, can you tell us in lay terms what a golem is?" said Torie.

"A golem is a creature traditionally made of clay and brought to life by magic," said Opal. "They are used to perform their creator's bidding."

"Or they can act as protectors," said Jasmin.

"True," said Opal. "The question is, what was this one made for?"

"He seems pretty protective of Myra Simms' body."

Torie paced the floor, arms folded, one hand cupping her chin. "So Mr. Simms isn't real? He's something that someone made...with magic?"

"Making a golem is advanced magic," said Opal. "It is beyond the skill of all but the most advanced practitioners of the arts."

"So, who could have done this?" asked Torie.

Opal pointed to the dead woman on the bed. "You're looking at her."

"What? Are you saying this...teacher, was a masters-level witch?" said Jasmin.

"Not at all," replied Opal. "There is not a whiff of power coming from that body. Even the ambient air in this home has no residual magic. But golems only respond to the orders of their creators. He was holding her deceased form, guarding it if you will. There is no mistake who created it. Elric, is this the same man you saw with her on the street?"

The werewolf nodded, squinting to get a good look at the man. "Yes. that's definitely him."

"If he was following her then she was his creator," said Opal. "We just need to figure out how she did it."

"Well, at least we know why there is so much of that weird mud back there," said Jasmin. "She obviously used it to remake her husband and bring him back from the dead."

Opal wagged one finger at her sister, shaking her head. "No. This is not her husband reanimated. This is a lifeless, soulless husk, devoid of reason and emotion. It is a stand-in for the real thing, but nothing more."

"Maybe that's why she made him," said Torie. "They were together a long time, living here in this house, probably not spending any time apart. When he died, it was like losing a piece of herself. She must have been overcome with grief to do something like this."

"But how did she do it?" asked Jasmin. "Where did she find enchanted mud? Even after crafting this thing, how did she bring it to life?"

Torie snapped her finger in excitement. "Remember what the hunter said? That the humans in town were doing things...playing with magic they had no business messing with. Elric, you said the same thing. Maybe this was part of it."

"There's a huge difference between animating a vacuum

cleaner and bringing a statue made of mud to life," said Jasmin. "Still, I guess it wouldn't hurt to look further into it. It's not like we have any other leads at the moment."

"What about Max?" asked Elric. He was starting to pace in frustration. "The woman we found here is not going to be of any help, and this...golem can't tell us anything. This was little more than a dead end. We could have used this time to track the hunter and find Max."

"Hey, it's okay. We are certainly going to find Max. That's a given," said Torie.

"If he's still alive," said Opal, half to herself and half to the group.

"He's alive," said Elric, glaring at the witch. "He was my alpha once. We may not be as close as we once were, but I'd know if he were dead."

Opal's head snapped around as she studied Elric. "Of course! Shifters of a same species are typically connected by a shared bond through the magic that created them. That's never truer than with werewolves. And you two were alpha and beta...that makes you even more connected. Can you sense Max right now?"

A look of confusion passed over Elric as he considered her words.

"Actually, no, I can't feel him anymore."

"What about when you fought at the house?" Opal continued.

Elric thought about it for a moment. "Now that you mention it, no. Even though I was fighting him, it was like..."

"He wasn't really there," said Opal, finishing his thought. "Just like with the golem, right?"

"Yes. In the heat of the battle I didn't notice it. But it

was like Max wasn't even there. He didn't register on any of my senses except for what I could physically see."

Jasmin's eyes widened as she started to grasp where her sister was going. She moved over to stand in front of the golem, slowly reaching for him.

"The hunter had to be controlling Max with some type of divinity object. It's the only thing magical that she possessed and only magic could bend a werewolf's will to hers. That means..." she began to pat the pockets of the golem, feeling first those on his plaid shirt and then moving to his loose-fitting khaki pants, "this golem could possess the same type of object. Something that not only gives him life, but also renders him invisible to magic and any mystically enhanced senses."

She finished patting him down and stepped back, perplexed.

"Nothing," she said, folding her arms dejectedly.

"Hold on," said Opal. "There's nothing *on* him...but he's made of mud. Maybe what we are looking for is *inside* of him."

"How do we find something like that?" asked Jasmin.

"I know," said Torie. "We take him to the hospital. They have equipment there that can look inside the body, right? Surely someone there can help us?"

"Great idea," said Opal. "Let's head over there. You," she pointed at Torie, "bring the golem."

"Wait...what? Why me?"

Opal grinned. "Oh, didn't I tell you? It's *your* magic that animated this lump of mud. That makes *you* his new master."

Chapter Seventeen

The ride to the hospital was uncomfortable, to say the least. Opal and Jasmin sat up front while Torie crammed into the backseat with Elric and the golem, who sat silently between them.

"So, I don't understand how you could just forget to tell me my magic is inside this man. What does that even mean?" asked Torie.

"So how do you think she stumbled across the mud?" Jasmin said to Opal, ignoring Torie.

"No idea. But she also had to know the mud alone wouldn't be enough. I'm betting that's where a divinity object of some sort must have come into play," replied Opal. "She wasn't a witch, so she had to use a magically charged item to jump start him."

"That, combined with the mud, was enough to make a golem. Interesting. And the mud? You think that has something to do with the hunter being able to control Max? Fionna said he stepped in some and it freaked him out."

Opal nodded. "That's a theory. But who knows for sure."

"Hello? I'm here too, you know," said Torie.

"And what about the smaller golem that was on the table. What do you think that was about?" said Opal, again speaking to Jasmin.

"Maybe she was making some kind of messed-up golem family?" Jasmin replied before turning to face Torie. "And he isn't a man."

"What?" said Torie, slightly annoyed.

"You said your magic is inside 'this man'. It isn't a man, and you need to remember that." She gave the golem a look of disdain before turning back around in her seat. "As for how your magic got in it…well…that's anyone's guess."

"Or not," said Opal. "I have a theory. One that the Elders we visited on the astral plane pretty much confirmed." Their car was eerily silent as all eyes, with the exception of the golem's, fell on the witch. ". Remember, magic can't be destroyed. Torie didn't *lose* her powers, she gave them up; tossed them away like so much garbage."

"Hey, that hurts," said Torie.

"Sorry. I'm not one for mincing words. But it should hurt. You're a witch; those powers were your birthright. And yet you threw them away."

"I had a reason," Torie said.

"Yes, to save a newborn from a warlock. No one is faulting you or saying you made the wrong choice."

"Really? Cos that's exactly what it sounds like to me."

"Opal, that isn't fair," said Jasmin. "You weren't here. The sacrifice Torie made saved all of us. You can't come in and armchair quarterback by telling us what we should have done differently."

Opal didn't speak but glanced briefly at her sister and nodded.

"You're right. That isn't my place. What's done is done. I apologize."

Torie looked from one sister to the next before releasing a sigh. "Well, of course I accept. Could you please go on with your theory?"

"I think that when you...relinquished your powers, they had no place to go. Normally, when a witch passes on, her power returns to the source of our magic naturally. Meaning it returns to Mother Nature...Earth, if you will. There it is recycled into the natural course of things; becoming one with the universe until it is time to be tapped again and given to a new witch. But in your case, you didn't die. Your magic was forced out and into the world in a most unnatural way. It had no meaning, no place to go; so, it made its own course. Settling into the environment around us."

"Wild magic," said Jasmin.

Opal nodded. "Wild magic. Free roaming hex power, looking for a home. I'm betting that is what Myra Simms used to create this golem."

Torie sat back, shocked at what she was hearing. Elric slipped a hand over hers and gave her a gentle, reassuring caress.

"Hey, this is good news, right?" he said.

"It is if we can figure out how to get the magic back into Torie," replied Opal.

"Shouldn't be hard," said Jasmin. "I mean, it belongs to her, right?"

"Correction. It used to. She gave it away. Now it belongs to whoever has claimed it. And since this golem can't talk, it was claimed by his dead wife," said Opal.

Torie remained silent, unsure what, if anything, she could do. She glanced at the silent golem sitting next to her and wondered how her magic could have created something like this. It was not something she had ever imagined doing, and yet here it was. She closed her eyes and placed a hand on his, trying to probe with her mind and heart.

Nothing.

Why was it that Elric and Opal could sense her magic inside him, but she could not? Had she truly closed herself off to what had become the most important part of her being? And if that was the case, how would she ever regain that which was lost?

She opened her eyes to see Opal watching her. The witch just smiled and nodded. It was as if she knew what Torie was trying to do and in some small way was encouraging her.

"We're here," said Jasmin, easing the vehicle into the parking lot of the community hospital that sat just outside of Singing Falls.

"Not here," said Opal. "This is the emergency department entrance. No way we can even get out of the car without being noticed. Take us around the back. Try to find a loading dock."

Jasmin did as she asked and slowly maneuvered her way to a darkened side lot next to an empty dock with a gray, metallic door with a single, dim light overhead.

"This will work," said Opal. "Hopefully there are no cameras."

"This is a hospital. There are probably cameras everywhere," said Torie, glumly. "How do we get in? And even if we get in, where are we going and what do we do when we get there?"

She was starting to fidget. Her nerves were strung and

the more she thought about it, the less she liked this plan of action.

"Just calm down," said Jasmin as she took out her phone. "Fionna is here with Glen, remember? I'm going to give her a call and ask her to come meet us at the dock."

"Are you sure she'll be able to find us?" asked Torie.

"Of course she will. When they were first dating, she used to spend a lot of time here with Glen. They were sneaking in and out of every closet in this building. She knows it like the back of her hand." She gave Torie a look, her brows furrowing. "What's going on with you? Are you okay?"

"I'm fine. I just don't like hospitals. They freak me out."

She wasn't lying; she just wasn't voicing the full truth.

Jasmin turned around in her seat and spoke quickly on the phone before clicking it off.

"Okay, Fionna's going to open the door and meet us. Let's go."

They made their way out of the car and towards the concrete steps that led to the loading dock. Torie gripped the golem's hand and pulled him along.

"We look like bandits standing here," said Torie as they waited for Fionna to open the door.

"I don't know what kind of bandits you've met, but trust me, we ain't it," said Opal.

The sound of metal scraping against metal rang out as Fionna lifted the latch on the other side of the door and swung it open for them.

"What are you guys doing here?" she asked, eyes wide. "And who is that?" She narrowed her eyes at the golem trailing along behind Torie as they entered the building.

She leaned in and sniffed him.

"More like *what* is that?" she mumbled.

"First things first. How is Glen?" Torie asked.

Fionna took a deep breath. "Her liver is bruised pretty bad from the beating she took. But nothing that a few weeks' rest won't heal. She was lucky."

"Is she awake?" asked Jasmin.

"She is. Well, she's in and out, but she's definitely out of the woods. They want her to stay here for observation for a couple more days, then I'm taking her home."

Everyone breathed a collective sigh of relief.

"So, what are you guys doing here with…him?" Fionna asked.

"He's a golem," said Opal. "And I think he has something buried inside him that we can use to find our friend, the hunter, and Max as well."

Elric perked up at the mention of his friend. "Really?"

"I think so. As we said, his wife wasn't a witch, so she would not have had the magic to bring this lump of mud to life. That means he has an external source of magic."

"Like a battery?" said Fionna.

"Exactly. Only this battery was charged by Torie's magic. I believe that her magic, once it left her, attached itself to certain properties and settled in them."

Jasmin snapped her fingers. "Crystals!"

"Yep. That's my guess," said Opal.

"Okay slow down. You're both way ahead of me," said Torie. "What crystals?"

Jasmin turned to her friend. "Certain types of minerals and natural elements can be conduits for magic. The most common are rock crystals. That's why so many witches use crystal balls and healing crystals. Magic seeps into them over time, and witches can draw on that stored power to perform all kinds of feats."

"Crystals like the ones you brought to my house for me

to use?" said Torie. "But I wasn't able to access the power in them."

"Yes. But I had no idea at the time that you were completely bereft of your powers. They respond to witches. Your hex power was gone, so that explains why you couldn't get the slightest response from them."

"So what changes?" Torie asked.

"Well, now that we know the problem…maybe we can come up with a different angle to attack it from," said Opal.

Elric cleared his throat. "Not to interrupt, but how do these crystals help to find Max?"

"Divinity objects operate the same way. They are just objects that store magic and are used at the discretion of the one wielding them. When the hunter showed up at the bar, she was wielding a small gold chain as a divinity object. But a divinity object like that has a very specific purpose. I'm betting she didn't have one that would allow her to enslave a werewolf."

"So that means she must have stumbled over a crystal, just like this golem's wife did. She used it to do her bidding, namely, take control of Max," said Jasmin.

"But wait…I thought you said that these crystals only worked for witches? How is a hunter, and, for that matter, a town full of humans, able to wield them?" asked Fionna.

"Good question," said Opal. "I think the difference comes in the form of the magic that is in the crystals. In the wild, that magic accumulates little by little over great periods of time. It comes from natural sources; the decay of Mother Nature, the ambient energy that is created by the natural life and death cycle of living creatures. But in this case, it was a sudden rush of magical power that soaked the area; it wasn't part of the natural order. So that is allowing anyone who happens to stumble across it to access it."

Torie looked at the golem. In many ways what Opal had just said made sense. But if that were the case, why wouldn't she be able to access her own magic? Why was it so cut off from her? That thought made her more afraid than she had been when she thought her hex powers were gone for good.

"So how can I help?" asked Fionna.

"We need to test that theory. We need a way to look inside him," said Opal.

Fionna thought for a moment. "Well, the X-ray technologist on duty is a hawk shifter who owes Glen a favor. Maybe we could sneak him down to radiology and he could have a look inside him…it. Whatever," said Fionna.

"Now that sounds like an excellent idea," said Jasmin, giving Fionna a big smile. "Why don't you lead the way?"

They made their way through the maze of back hallways that skirted the emergency department and the intake reception desks, eventually emptying out into a corridor that was awash in yellowish light and lined with huge, blue linen carts draped with green cloth meant to keep the towels and cloth gowns clean. Sitting between two of the bins was a metal stretcher with a thin, gray pad.

"Here, put him on this," Fionna said, pulling the stretcher away from the wall. She then went to one of the laundry bins and retrieved a sheet. "Hopefully he'll just look like any other patient being wheeled into X-ray if we're seen."

Torie led the golem to the stretcher and persuaded him to climb on board. Once he was resting on his back, they covered him with the sheet and Fionna pushed him towards a set of free-swinging double doors marked "Radiology".

As luck would have it, there were no other patients or employees in the hall, and they moved easily through a couple of corridors until they came to a desk with a large man perched behind it. He stood, towering over them and looked suspiciously at the man on the stretcher and then at Fionna. Finally, he glanced at the company that filed in behind her and frowned.

"Uh uh, not at all," he said, his voice gruff and low. "Whatever you're doing, Fi, I want nothing to do with it."

"Gerald," she replied, her voice taking on a familial and pleading tone, "I just need this one favor. You owe me and you know that."

"Girl, I don't owe you shit. I owe Glen...but you ain't her."

"C'mon, man, if she were here, Glen would be asking you to help us out. But she's not here. She's lying in a bed upstairs after being critically injured. And what we are asking can help us find out why she was hurt...and catch the person who put her here."

Gerald gave her a steely-eyed stare before rolling his eyes.

"Fine. But if anything gets me fired, I'm coming to live rent free with you. What do you need?"

Jasmin pushed in front of Fionna. "We need you to X-ray this...man. Head to toe. We are looking for a foreign object."

"What kind of foreign object?" asked Gerald.

"Anything that shouldn't be there. Can you do that?" asked Jasmin.

The technologist nodded and moved over to the foot of the stretcher. "I'll take him in. This might take a few minutes, so you all wait out here."

Torie, Jasmin and Opal moved to sit on chairs that were arranged along the wall opposite the desk where Gerald had been sitting.

Elric didn't move, giving the X-ray tech a stormy look.

"Why can't we go in there with you?" he asked. "Maybe because you're going to make off with whatever you find inside him."

"What? What are you talking about?" said Gerald.

"He's right," said Fionna, moving to stand next to Elric. "This is important. It will help me to protect Glen. One of us should keep an eye on you." Her hands were balled into fists as she took a step towards her friend.

"Hey, I don't need you stepping in to help me. Mind your business," said Elric. His voice was low and impatient, and he stared hard at Fionna.

"Actually, I don't need either of you watching over me telling me how to do *my job*," said Gerald. His eyes flashed dangerously, flickering yellow briefly in the dim overhead light.

"What are you going to do to stop us?" said Elric. "Flap us to death with your wings?"

"Hey, hey, hey," said Jasmin, eying the three shifters. "What is going on here?"

"What's going on is someone needs to teach this hawk some manners when he addresses a shifter above his weight class," said Elric, advancing on Gerald.

"Elric," said Torie, rising from her chair. "What has gotten into you?"

"Oh no," said Opal.

Before she could say anything more, all hell broke loose as the three shifters charged one another.

Chapter Eighteen

Torie screamed as pandemonium broke out.

In an instant, Elric had vaulted across the stretcher and was pummeling Gerald with his fists. Fionna let out a screech that nearly pierced Torie's ears as she darted around and leapt on Elric's back, grabbing a handful of hair to pull his head back.

That gave Gerald the opening he needed to throw his one punch, landing a blow to Elric's midsection that knocked the breath out of him. As he staggered backwards, Fionna leapt off his back and threw a series of high kicks at Gerald's face. He parried them, then, moving swifter than even Fionna expected, lunged forward and grabbed her by the throat.

Grabbing the much larger man's arm, Fionna swung her legs up and around his shoulders, seeking to close them on his neck. Before she could complete the deadly move, Elric had recovered sufficiently enough to throw himself against both of their entangled bodies. Lifting them from the ground he twisted, throwing them behind the desk.

A high-pitched screech rang out from behind the desk, and suddenly, a large hawk appeared. Wings stretched outward as Gerald completed his shift. In response, Elric dropped into his wolf form, baring his fangs as he settled his weight on his hind legs, preparing to spring at the hawk shifter.

Before he could attack, a wall of blue light separated the two of them. Jasmin held up both hands, her magic flowing forward to create a divide.

Fionna was not trapped by the mystic wall, however, and wheeled on Jasmin. Baring her teeth, she leapt at the witch, only to be caught in midair by a wave of white power cast from Opal.

"No, not them," shouted Torie, cupping her hands around her mouth to be heard over the din of shifters hell-bent on killing anyone they could get their claws into. "The golem! Cast a shield around him!"

Opal nodded in understanding.

"Sorry, Fionna," she said. She gave her magic a small mental nudge, just enough to send the squirrel shifter bouncing away from her. Before Fionna could regain her balance, Opal turned and cast a shimmering white globe around the golem, enveloping him completely.

Almost at once, the three shifters ceased their struggling. Elric and Gerald regained their human forms, each looking dazed and confused as they took in the scene around them.

"What...what just happened?" said Elric.

"You just went full-blown wolf and tried to have some bird for dinner," said Jasmin, nodding at Gerald.

"Oh no," said Elric, looking around for Torie. "Did I hurt anyone?"

"No, but not for lack of trying," said Opal.

Fionna approached, shaking her head as if to clear

cobwebs. "I am so sorry, Opal…I could see what I was doing, but I couldn't stop myself. I was just so angry all of a sudden; to the point that I lost all control."

"Same here," said Gerald. "That was an awful feeling; something I never want to experience again."

"It was the golem," said Torie. "He was also at the bakery and the bar, and he created the same affect among the shifters there."

"But how?" asked Elric. "I sat right next to him on the car ride over. I didn't feel anything like what just happened."

"Yes, but you were the only shifter around him then," said Jasmin. "It could be that when more than one of you from different shifter families comes into contact with him…or more likely with the magic that is powering him, it triggers this violent reaction until he is removed from the equation."

"I've heard of weirder things," said Opal as she walked over to the encased golem to stare at him. "Shifters are creatures of magic. Some of the oldest creatures in the supernatural world; second only to vampires in their creation. The magic that flows in you is instinctual; part of nature. What is in this golem is something not meant to occur in nature. It's disrupting the natural order."

"But…if it's my magic, why would it behave like this?" asked Torie. "I don't harbor any ill will towards shifters."

"I don't think you have to," said Opal. "It may be your magic, but it is unconstrained now. It is wild magic; and wild magic with no master brings chaos."

"The quicker we get a peek at what's inside him, and maybe get it out, the better," said Jasmin. "What if he isn't the only one that this could happen with? Elric said the humans are playing with magic…what if the same thing happens with them? Or worse, it infects the rest of the shifters in the community?"

"Wouldn't they already feel the effects?" said Fionna. "I mean, it hit me so fast, with no warning. What if it's already happening?"

Jasmin was shaking her head. "Doubtful. We're in the closest hospital to town and it's very quiet so far. My bet is this is a unique case. Golems are not found in nature; they are made. By skilled wielders of magic. This one was made by a human using borrowed magic. It is disrupting everything. That's why it is causing havoc when it encounters the shifters. At least, that's my theory."

Opal nodded. "It's as good as anything else we have to go on. Plus, containing it seems to have broken the violence, so that lends credence to your theory."

"So, what now?"

"Same plan," said Opal. "Gerald here takes it in for X-rays. Only this time I'm going with him to keep the room sealed up tight so no energy from him can leak out."

Torie nodded, unable to find the words to express what she was feeling. She watched as Gerald pushed the stretcher into the room, followed closely by Opal as she maintained the integrity of her shields. As they disappeared behind the swinging doors, she moved back to the wall and plopped down onto one of the chairs.

Jasmin made her way to the chair next to her.

"You okay? You've seemed off, and I know it's not just being in this hospital."

Torie sighed and looked at her friend.

"I was just getting to the point that I accepted the loss of my magic. I was almost at peace with it. But then, I let myself get caught up in hope, only to find out that...that what I did was so bad. I'm responsible for those hurt shifters in town. I'm responsible for the creation of that golem. I mean, what must that poor woman have gone through to want to do something like that?"

"Hurt. She went through love and loss, Torie. That kind of pain…who knows what it did to her? But think of it like this; your act allowed her to spend some time with something, with a remembrance of her husband."

Torie looked at her, trying to force a smile. "And who knows? Maybe what I did is the reason your daughter is here."

Jasmin looked away. Now it was her turn to hide her emotions.

Torie reached out and gave her hand a squeeze. "Why didn't you ever tell me?"

"I was ashamed. I tucked that shame so far back into my mind…I just wanted to forget it. I had no idea it would come walking into my life as a grown-up assassin-for-hire one day."

"We can fix this," said Torie. "All of it. Maybe this happened to me because I don't deserve my magic."

"Then by that logic, are you saying my daughter is here because I didn't deserve her?"

"No. I think that is because you *do* deserve her. She didn't kill us, remember? For that matter, she didn't kill Elric and maybe hasn't killed Max yet either. Maybe deep down inside, she's not what she pretends to be, and part of her wants us to realize that."

Jasmin looked at her and smiled, slowly shaking her head.

"You are something else, you know that? After all the horrors you've seen you still want to see the good in people."

Torie nodded. "Of course. If you go around looking for darkness, that's all you'll find."

"You know, if this doesn't work out; if you don't get your powers back, I want you to know you still have a home here."

Torie laughed. "Technically, I don't have a home any longer. Pretty sure mine is now condemned."

Jasmin looked at her, her face deadly serious. "You have a home with me. Always. I have more room than I know what to do with."

"Thank you, Jasmin. I mean that." She felt a lump form in her throat. Her friend's words were spoken from the heart and were so pure and authentic it made Torie's heart ache. "But…we'll see."

Jasmin knew not to push it. Instead, she elbowed Torie and nodded in Elric's direction. He was pacing in front of the desk in a way that made the women think of a caged animal.

"He's worried about Max," said Jasmin.

"As am I. We need to find him. Soon."

Jasmin nodded before leaning in to whisper in Torie's ear. "You know I want all the details, right? I mean, I need to know all the nitty gritty. I've always heard that wolves are the best lovers."

Torie looked at her friend in shock as her face turned beet-red.

Jasmin howled with laughter, throwing her head back. "I knew it! At least tell me he was better than your ex-husband. Cos, really that's all that matters."

Torie tried to stifle a laugh at her friend. "Well, *anything* was better than that."

"Yeah, he looked pretty tame. Like missionary all the way I bet."

Torie tried to feign shock but could only laugh even harder.

"How sad," said Jasmin. "What a waste. My motto is that anyone who can't see beyond that tired old position does not deserve all the sex I have to offer."

"Jasmin! Is this the right time for such talk?" She cast her eyes down as guilt crept over her.

Jasmin placed a hand on her friend's shoulder and made her look at her. Then, she placed the palm of her hand on Torie's chest.

"Do you feel that, Torie? It's joy, and life, and hope, and happiness. Even if only for a moment. You felt it. I'm betting there is plenty more where that came from. And you know what? That all came from inside you. It wasn't magic: it was Torie. Don't feel guilty for allowing yourself to feel good. Remember that in the days to come; no matter what happens."

Again, Torie felt at a loss for words. She could not imagine feeling any more accepted than she did at that moment. She realized how lucky she was to have a friend like Jasmin, and looking up at Elric, she knew that even though she might be powerless, she would help move heaven and earth to help him. Elric stopped his pacing and looked over at her, arching an eyebrow.

It was times like this that she really missed their telepathic rapport. But even without it, she had a feeling he knew exactly what she was thinking.

The doors swung open as Gerald pushed the stretcher through, followed by Opal and Fionna. Even though the glow of magic still encapsulated the golem, Torie saw Elric take a few steps back from them, isolating himself behind the desk.

"Well, did you find anything?" asked Torie, jumping to her feet.

"Oh, you could say that," said Gerald. He stopped rolling the stretcher and picked up a couple of sheets of X-ray film that was resting on top of the golem. He held them up to the light and motioned for Torie and Jasmin to come take a look.

"What are we looking at?" asked Torie.

"This is his abdomen," he held the film up and indicated an outline of structures shown in varying shades of black and gray.

"They just look like a hodgepodge of weird shapes," said Jasmin. "Not like the X-rays that are always hanging up in the background of *Grey's Anatomy*."

"Exactly," said Gerald. "That's because there is nothing inside him. Just a bunch of stuff that seems to be free-floating. There is the basic outline of a skeleton, but that's it. He has no internal organs at all."

"Well, so much for finding something hidden in all that," said Torie dejectedly.

"That's what I was thinking," said Gerald, "but then I noticed this." He held the film back up and pointed to a small speck of white to one side of the film. "See how this shows up whiter than everything else around it? Well, the denser something is, the less it's being penetrated by X-ray; meaning the harder it is."

"Like a piece of rock or crystal," said Jasmin, her eyes wide.

"Exactly. So I took a second image and cranked up the radiation to the point that it blacked out everything else; but this thing still showed just as bright as a little sun." He held up a second film, this one nearly black with only the white substance clearly outlined. It was the size of a quarter and could clearly be seen floating in the blackness of the image. "This was just to demonstrate that whatever it is, it's not your normal foreign body. My guess is this is exactly what you are looking for."

"Has to be it," said Jasmin. "Question is, how do we get it out?"

"That's easy," came a voice from behind them. "I use this."

The hunter was standing just outside the main corridor looking at the group of friends. In her hands, she twirled a silver blade that gave off an ominous hum as it spun around her fingers.

Chapter Nineteen

Tension and fear crept through the space.

Opal summoned ghostly tentacles that wrapped themselves around her as she backed up to where Jasmin and Torie stood. Jasmin called on her full hex power in the form of glowing spheres that flashed around her fists and placed herself between the hunter and Torie. A growl echoed from behind the desk as Elric shifted into his full wolf form. On his back crouched Fionna in her squirrel form. The two of them were poised to spring, not taking their eyes off the hunter.

"What's going on? Who is this?" asked Gerald cautiously. "Damnit, Fionna I told you not to bring your mess to my house like this." Unsure of what to do, he turned and ran back through the double doors that separated them from the radiology department.

"Easy there," said the hunter. "I am not here to fight."

"That knife says otherwise," said Opal.

"No, this was just to get your attention." She stopped twirling the knife and slowly re-sheathed it back into the leather holster strapped to her hip. "You have something I want. Actually, you have two somethings I want." She cut her eyes to Elric behind the desk. He growled, baring an impressive set of fangs. "Easy there, Cujo. My knife is made of pure silver. It's sheathed, but I'm willing to bet that no matter how fast you are, I'm faster. Why don't you shift back to human form and move over next to your friends so we can all chat?"

Torie peeked from behind Jasmin and motioned for Elric to come over to them. Reluctantly, the werewolf shifted back to human form, as did Fionna. Together the two of them walked slowly across the room to where their friends stood.

"That's better," the hunter said. She walked casually to the desk and jumped up onto it, sitting cross-legged. She stared at the golem on the stretcher for a moment before focusing her gaze on everyone across from her. "I have to say, seeing you all together like this is strange, to say the least. I mean, witches, werewolves, weresquirrel and a… witch has been? Is that what you are?" she said to Torie.

No one responded, so the hunter just shrugged before continuing.

"You know why it's so weird to me? Because you're all supposed to be enemies. Witches are not friends with shifters. And they certainly don't sleep with them! And you," she pointed at Fionna, "little tree rat, they definitely eat your kind. I don't get what's happening here. And the only witch I've ever known was definitely a loner. I mean, the only reason you all would be pals would be to steal magic from one another."

"We aren't like that," said Torie. "We are like family to one another."

The hunter flinched and her face grew hard as she stared at Jasmin. "I take it you recognized the locket?"

Jasmin swallowed hard and nodded. "If this is about me, let's talk about…"

The hunter held up a stiff hand to cut her off.

"Nah, there is nothing to talk about. I'll get to you in a minute." Her eyes bored into Jasmin and her hand twitched as it rested next to the hilt of her blade.

"Why don't you tell us what you want?" said Torie, seeking to defuse the situation as much as possible.

"Where's Max?" asked Elric, his eyes glowing as he stared at the hunter.

"Oh, he's safe. I'll take you to him in just a bit."

"No one's going anywhere," said Opal. "I'm not sure what you're after here, but we have numbers and strength on our side. And you're not catching us off guard this time."

"Well, look at you, Auntie. Being all big and tough. I've done my research on you. Have you told them why you're really up here? Cos it sure as hell ain't to cure a witch who lost her powers." She glanced over at Jasmin. "What did she tell you her little smoke monster is? Cos trust me; it's not a familiar."

Opal flinched and could feel Torie's eyes on her but refused to break the hunter's gaze.

"You seem to know an awful lot about supernaturals and witches," said Torie. "Why is that?"

"It's literally my business. I need to know what I'm up against, so I make it my business to learn. Anytime I go up against a super I like to know their strengths and their weaknesses. How do you think I captured your buddy Max?"

At the mention of his friend, Elric growled, his body shifting into his hybrid form. He bared his fangs and flexed the muscles of his arms, causing dagger-like claws to descend.

The hunter immediately uncoiled, standing up on the desk in one smooth motion.

"Do you think I'm here alone?" she said, her voice half mocking and half threatening. "You're right, you do outnumber me, and as much as it might be fun to take you all on, I really don't have time for that."

She held up a hand and made a beckoning motion. From the shadows of the hall, three men appeared, each carrying a wicked-looking gun. Torie had no idea what kind of weapons they were but they reminded her of the ones that were always on the news after a domestic shooting incident. They raised the weapons and aimed them at the group of friends.

"Recognize them, Elric?" the hunter asked.

The wolf only growled, his eyes fixed on the men.

"Elric, who are those men?" Torie pressed.

When he didn't answer, the hunter laughed and cleared her throat, hopping from the desk to the floor.

"They are some old friends of his. They work for his ex-boss down in Trinity Cove. You see, once I realized there was a lot more going on up here in this sleepy little village than I had been made aware of, I decided to call in some reinforcements."

"Please, there is no need for this," said Torie, her heart racing. "This doesn't need to happen. Let's just talk about this. You said you wanted something else, what is it?"

The hunter flashed them a brilliant smile and pointed. First to Elric, and then to the golem.

Torie swallowed hard and placed a hand on Elric's arm. She could feel the wolf trembling as his breathing increased.

He was on the verge of a full shift, and Torie sensed that if he did, he would charge the hunter.

"They're not going anywhere," said Jasmin. "Why don't you and I go somewhere and talk about this…"

"No, witch, we will not. You are no use to me. The wolf has a price on his head, so I need him. As for the clay man…I want to remove his battery and add it to my collection. I'm betting a divinity object like that will fetch a pretty price on the open market."

"He won't go with you, whatever is in him is from——" Torie started to say but was quickly cut off by a look from Jasmin.

The hunter looked at the two of them. "From what? Finish your sentence."

When Torie didn't speak, the hunter removed the silver blade from her hilt. "Fine. Whatever. I'm losing patience, so here's how this will go. Elric, push the golem over to us, and then put your arms behind your back to be shackled." She reached behind her under her jacket and withdrew a set of handcuffs. "They're pure silver, so you won't be able to break them." She tossed the handcuffs to one of the men holding a gun.

When Elric didn't move, she nodded to another of the men. He flipped a switch on the gun and a red dot appeared on Torie's forehead. She had seen enough movies to know what that flash of red was.

"Okay. Now that everyone is paying attention, listen up cos I'm only going to say this once. I know ya'll are old, so I'll say it loud." She cleared her throat and proceeded to raise her voice. "Elric, either you do what I just said, or I order Jimmy here to shoot your squeeze in the head. Now, I wonder if dear old Jasmin there could stop the bullet with her magic. Maybe, though I'm not entirely sure your shields can stop bullets. At any rate, even if you stopped *one*, I'm willing to bet you can't stop them *all*."

At her words, the two remaining men raised their sights and shined two more laser dots on Torie.

"And I wonder which of you it would hurt more?" the hunter said. "Wolves mate for life, am I right, Elric? But I'm willing to bet it would hurt dear old Jazzy almost as much. Maybe more."

"You wouldn't do that," said Jasmin. "I know you aren't a cold-blooded killer."

The hunter's eyes grew hard as she glared at Jasmin. "How can you know what I am or am not? You don't *know* me. You had your chance, and you threw it, and me, away. So you keep believing that you know me while you're scooping up what's left of your best friend there."

She turned back to the men with her and nodded. There was an audible click as they each slid the safeties to the off position, their arms tensing as they moved a finger towards the trigger.

"No, stop!" said Elric. He threw himself in front of the women, shifting back to his human form. "I'll go with you. Just don't hurt anyone."

Before Torie or Jasmin could object, he moved over to the stretcher and pushed it forward, close to the hunter and her men. Then he placed his arms behind him and presented his backside to the man with the cuffs. His eyes pleaded with Torie and Jasmin not to try anything. The pain of the silver snapping around his wrists made him wince and he nearly buckled under the weakness the cuffs caused him.

"And now, just because I don't quite trust you, even in those cuffs…" said the hunter as she walked up to the wolf. She removed a collar with a red gem dangling from the inside of her leather jacket and snapped it around his neck before anyone could protest.

Elric's eyes flared yellow for a brief second and he staggered backwards before righting himself. His body strangely rigid, his eyes focused on nothing.

"What did you do?" demanded Torie, trying to move past Jasmin to get to Elric. The appearance of a red dot in the center of her chest stopped her in her tracks.

"Oh calm down. It's nothing," said the hunter. "I put one around Max too, and it made a world of difference in his behavior." She winked at them and laughed as she and her men began to back away, one of them pushing the golem. "Put the clay man in the back of the van and lock Cujo in the cage."

As they walked away, she turned to face the women, her eyes looking around.

"Where's the tree-rat?"

Torie and Jasmin looked around. At some point during the confrontation, Fionna had disappeared from view.

The hunter squinted at them. "No matter. She is simply showing her true colors. Run and hide is what small shifters do."

She turned her back and beckoned to her men to follow her as she strolled down the hall. "And just in case you get any ideas, try something and I'll make sure the first bullet fired by my men goes into the wolf." She stopped and looked back at Opal. "And this isn't *Lost*. I better not look back and see any smoke monster following us."

With that, they were gone. The lingering sound of the squeaky stretcher wheels fading into nothingness as they disappeared down the long corridor and out of view.

Chapter Twenty

"Where the hell is Fionna?" Torie asked.

"No idea," said Jasmin, "but knowing her the way I do, I'm sure she's fine."

"We need to go," said Opal.

"No, what we need to do is find Fionna and then go after Elric," said Torie, turning on them. "I don't know what you're used to down in New Orleans, but here we take care of our friends."

She was too angry to regret what she said, even when she saw Opal flinch at her words.

"Look, I get it. I'm as pissed off about all of this as you, but we need to regroup," said Jasmin, taking Torie by the arm. "We need to go back to the house and devise next steps."

"Not without me," came a voice from behind them.

They turned to see Glen propped against the door jam leading into the radiology department. She held herself up with one arm, using the other to hold against her abdomen.

"Glen!" shouted Torie, racing over to support her and ease her onto a chair.

"No way," said Jasmin. "You're going right back upstairs and getting into bed. What are you even doing down here?"

She grunted in response, holding her stomach. "Gerald just came by my room. Said there was a commotion down here involving Fionna. Where is she and what happened?"

Jasmin and Torie exchanged looks.

"She's fine," said Torie. "We are looking after her, and as for what happened down here...well, it's hard to explain..."

"Supernatural stuff," said Jasmin, interjecting. "Nothing you need to worry about. We will take care of Fionna, you have my word, but you need to focus on taking care of you. Promise that once we get you back to your bed, you'll stay there. And in return, I promise to have Fionna back at your bedside as soon as possible."

Glen nodded between gasps of breath. Torie looked questioningly at Jasmin, but the witch ignored her. She took one of Glen's arms and gently placed it around her shoulder as she lifted her to her feet.

"Torie, help me get her back upstairs."

"We don't have time for this," started Opal. The look Jasmin gave her choked her words off.

"First we get Glen back to her room, then we plan our next steps," she said. "Do you have a problem with that, Opal?"

"No. Not at all, Jasmin."

They found a wheelchair and made their way back to Glen's room where they tucked her back into bed and reiterated that no matter what, Fionna was fine and she'd be checking in soon.

"In the meantime, you focus on getting some rest and getting better, alright?" said Jasmin, laying her hand on Glen's face as she leaned in and gave her a kiss on her forehead. Glen yawned, stretched a little, and drifted off almost immediately.

"Did you just...?" said Torie, pointing in disbelief at Glen.

"Nothing major. Just a slight healing spell for her body coupled with something to quiet her mind so she can rest."

Opal played her hands on her hips. "Now if *I* did that, you'd be ready to fight."

"You haven't earned your place to do that," replied Jasmin.

"Enough," said Torie, "let's get going. We have a lot to talk about and I don't want to do it here."

They made the drive back to Jasmin's house in near silence. As soon as they closed the front door, Torie collapsed on the couch.

"They have Elric," she said. "What are we going to do?"

Opal regarded her silently for a moment. "You're in love with him, aren't you?"

Torie didn't answer but felt tears welling up in her eyes. Everything she had experienced over the past forty-eight hours came bursting forth. Jasmin sat beside her, wrapping an arm around her and rocking her gently.

"Hey, it's going to be okay. We are going to get him and Max back and find Fionna," she said.

"And what *did* happen to Fionna? How could none of us have seen what happened to her? How could you tell Glen that she was fine like that? What if she isn't?"

"You saw yourself, the hunter didn't know where she went. That means she's still alive. And, if I know Fionna, she's probably somewhere about to make that hunter's life a little more miserable," said Jasmin.

Torie sat up, wiping her eyes. "And that. How can you just refer to your daughter as 'that hunter'? Doesn't it bother you? I'm a mess, I can't imagine what you must be feeling." She stood, pacing back and forth. "Of course, I wouldn't have to imagine if you'd just open up completely. I mean, I never even knew you had a sister, let alone a daughter."

Opal snickered and was quickly shut down by the look Torie gave her.

"And you," Torie said, "don't pretend that you can claim any high ground. What was that...your *niece*...talking about when she said that thing wasn't your familiar?"

Opal's face fell and she was unable to meet the gaze of the two women. Torie and Jasmin exchanged glances, each trying to encourage the other to push the matter.

Finally, Jasmin spoke up. "Opal, we haven't spoken in so long; let's not go back to that." She looked at Torie. "And I feel like I should have opened up to you sooner about everything. All I can say is I'm sorry. Some things are just too painful, and buried too deep, to see the light of day."

Tori took her friend's hand. "Pain is sometimes lessened if it's split among more than one person."

"Christ, *Hallmark* much?" said Opal snidely. "Fine. If you must know...it's not exactly my familiar. But I *am* familiar with it."

"What does that mean?" asked Torie.

Opal drew in a deep breath and plopped down in one of the chairs that sat opposite the couch.

"As you know, witches all have their specialties when it comes to magic. With me it was the spiritual plane that I connected with."

"Yeah, we learned that when we were children," said Jasmin.

"Yes, but what we weren't told was just how deep that connection is. Our hex magic is rooted deeply in the Astral plane, as you know. Well, in my case, that is the wellspring of my powers. I draw on the spirit world when I use my magic."

She took a deep breath and bit her lower lip before continuing.

"So, the first time my hex powers manifested, I was visited by small spirit creatures. They would show up when I used my power. The greater the magic I attempted, the larger the spirit that would visit me. Well, one night, I had a very fevered dream of a personal nature...if you know what I mean. But it wasn't like other dreams, it was so very real. Too real. I woke up and my room had been wrecked; furniture smashed, holes in the walls; it was terrible.

"And that was the first time I saw Metrian. He was at the end of the bed, watching me. Turns out, he was an incubus."

"What's that?" asked Torie.

Jasmin narrowed her eyes in anger.

"Are you telling me that your familiar is a sex ghost? You brought a sex ghost into my house, Opal?" She stood, jabbing a finger at her sister. "Oh my god...I changed clothes in the bedroom. I showered with the bathroom door open in my room! Has that thing been sneaking around watching me?" She wrapped her arms around herself, suppressing a shudder.

"No, of course not! Metrian isn't like that. He is attached to me, just like a familiar. That much was true."

"Why do you keep something like that around?" asked

Jasmin. "Can't you just…banish it back to wherever it came from?"

Opal looked away, puffing out her cheeks as she exhaled sharply. "Well, it's kind of like…I like having him around."

"Are you saying you're dating a…a sex ghost?" said Torie in a whisper. She looked around the room, wondering if they were being watched by the spirit at that moment.

Jasmin's jaw dropped. "Please tell me that isn't true."

"Okay, why are you judging me? She's dating a dog!"

"What? Elric's not a dog," Torie said sharply. "I mean… oh never mind what he is. And yes, he means a lot to me. That's why we need to get back to figuring out how to find him."

"Wait, are you comparing my friend's choice in boyfriend to what you're seeing? You're dating something that essentially slips into women's rooms at night and violates them," said Jasmin.

"That is not how it happened with Metrian," exclaimed Opal. "I called to him and invited him in!" She caught herself, snapping her mouth closed and folded her arms across her chest.

"What does that mean?" said Jasmin.

"Look, I had so many bad relationships. Just one right after the other. One day, after a particularly bad break up, I swore off men. I wished for something that would only be there when I wanted and would do the things to me that no man could do. It was a stupid thing to wish for. I really didn't think anything about it. But my damned hex powers sent that wish into the astral world and, well, Metrian answered. And you know what, I have never been happier!"

Jasmin looked at Torie before bursting out in laughter. She moved over to Opal and gave her a hug.

"Girl you go on with your Magic Wand. If you're happy

and you swear this thing isn't creeping on me in my house; go for it."

Opal relaxed in Jasmin's grip. "Are you sure? Just like that, you're good?"

"I just needed to make sure you were okay. Besides, I can't keep a man either, so who am I to judge?"

"Well, if you want, I can conjure you a—"

"No. Absolutely not," Jasmin interrupted, breaking the embrace and stepping away.

"Well, as much as I applaud our little breakthrough, we still have major problems," said Torie. "Namely, what do we do now to save Elric and Max? And maybe even Fionna."

"Not to pile onto that, but even after we find them, what do we do?" said Jasmin. "I mean, we are really out-numbered here. No offense, Torie, but only two of us have powers, and we are facing a hunter and two werewolves. Plus a pack of nasty little men and their guns."

"First things first," said Opal. "We find out where they are; and I think I can manage that."

She sat down on the floor, cross-legged, placing her hands palm-up on her knees.

"How? We need something that belongs to one of them to perform a tracking spell," said Jasmin.

"Which we don't have. But I planted something that just might help us," replied Opal. "Metrian."

Torie and Jasmin exchanged glances.

"I thought the hunter said not to have your sex ghost follow them," said Torie.

"And so he isn't. When they appeared, I had him merge into the body of the golem. If they are still with the golem, we can find them."

She closed her eyes and began to hum. Magic thrummed in the air. Even Torie could feel it vibrating and pulsing. The touch of it made her miss what she once was and long for forces she could no longer manipulate. She watched as Opal performed intricate hand motions in the air, ending with the formation of a box made by touching the tips of her forefingers and thumbs together. She opened her eyes, which had grown translucent with power, and peered into the space between her fingers.

"I see a lot of trees," she said.

"Well, we live on a mountain in the woods, so that's helpful," said Jasmin.

Opal ignored her, focusing instead on what only she could see. "There's a structure as well. It looks like a warehouse of some kind, that's been added onto a wooden and shingle structure. It spans a large creek. On one side is a huge gravel lot and the other, towering trees and darkness."

Jasmin snapped her fingers.

"That's the old Jensen Mill. Has to be. It's the only structure in the area that is built across the Stone Throw Creek. It used to be a paper mill back in the day. They built it over the creek because they used a waterwheel to help grind and pulp the wood into paper. It's so far off the beaten path, someone could hole up in there for months and no one would even suspect anything."

Torie leapt to her feet. "So, what are we waiting for?"

Opal and Jasmin exchanged looks. Torie wagged her finger, recognizing the look in their eyes.

"No way. I'm not sitting this out. I can't help but feel responsible for what has been going on, so I'm going to help. And so help me, Jasmin, if you put me to sleep " Torie said.

Jasmin held up both hands. "I would never do that to you. I also know there is no way to talk you out of this." She turned to her sister. "Do you have any ideas? Cos we are only going to get one shot at this; no backup will be coming."

Opal grinned. "Of course I have a plan. It might be a bit messy, and you're probably not going to like it, but it might just be the only way to save our friends and our own lives."

Chapter Twenty-One

The building that sprawled before them looked like a set piece from a made-for-television zombie apocalypse movie. The full moon shone through a cloudless night, illuminating the gravel lot that spread out in front of where they stood. It had been taken over by tall weeds and clumps of crab grass. There was no sign of cars, and Torie wondered where the vehicles the men had taken Elric away in were. The building beyond that was a two-story rectangular warehouse, with the upper level ringed by broken windows encased in rusting iron framework.

Torie could just make out the shingled form of the original structure grafted to the back of the warehouse. The three of them were quiet enough that they could just hear the whisper of running water from the creek that ran behind the old mill.

They had parked nearly a half-mile away and walked in on foot, not wanting to give their presence away to anyone inside the building. Opal had told them her plan on the way over, and she was right; no one liked it.

"Are you sure Fionna is inside?" queried Torie.

"Yes. According to Metrian, she's hiding inside the pocket of the golem. She must have shifted and scampered in there when those men with guns showed up," said Opal.

"Shhh." Jasmin held her finger to her lips, inviting them to speak in a whisper.

"They're six hundred yards away," whispered Opal. "What are we *shhhing* for?"

"Werewolves can hear a pin drop a half-mile away," said Jasmin. "I don't want to alert them to our arrival. She already has Max on her side, and if she's turned Elric as well…"

She didn't finish her sentence. She didn't have to. Getting caught in the open like this was not part of the craziness Opal had cooked up.

"Okay, so are we ready?" said Opal.

"No," said Jasmin, "but when has that ever stopped us before?" She gave Torie a friendly nudge with her elbow.

"Alright then," said Torie. "Here goes everything. You sure you want to split up like this?"

Opal nodded. "If they see all three of us, we lose the element of surprise and I may not be able to spring the trap. I can feel Metrian inside. I can make my way around back and come in that way. Warded by spirits I'll be practically invisible."

"Okay. We stick to the plan," said Torie. She and Jasmin gave Opal a quick hug and then started out across the gravel towards the front of the building.

"You know, if we were just going to waltz in the front door like this, why didn't we just drive up here? My knee is killing me from all this traipsing around. I'm too old for this."

"Hush. Age is all in the mind," said Torie.

"Maybe. But it's also in my knee and my back."

The front of the warehouse had multiple doors that were caving in or had been completely discarded. They picked one that was half ajar and squeezed into the musty space beyond. It smelled of peat moss and rotting wood. The hard floor beneath their feet was damp and slick in places where water had pooled, seeping up through cracks in the poured concrete.

Jasmin fumbled around in her pocket for a flashlight. While magic light would have been easier, but they didn't know what they might be dealing with just yet, so she didn't want to advertise her powers if she didn't have to. She swung the beam from dark corners to the floor in front of them as they made their way forward, listening for anything that might tell them where the hunter might be holed up.

"What if Opal was wrong and this isn't the place?" asked Torie.

"We have no reason to think she's wrong. Besides, we literally have no other ideas where to start looking. Plus, she doesn't live here, how would she have seen this mill before?"

"But where are the vehicles they were all driving? And this place is very creepy."

"Well, it's a lair for the bad guys. Were you expecting a basket of potpourri and some Dasani at the door?"

The strained sound of voices floated to their ears, freezing the two of them in place. Torie linked her arm through Jasmin's and together they headed in the direction the voices were coming from.

Ahead of them, the corridor they were walking down opened into a space where they could see flickers of light, and the voices became louder. They made out a woman's laughter, followed by that of several men.

"—And it doesn't matter how tough they are, silver

always puts them down," said a voice clearly as they crept closer. It was followed by a crackling sound and then a yelp and a whimper.

Elric.

Torie gripped Jasmin's arm harder as they continued toward the voices.

"I heard that an alpha and a beta were linked by some kind of supernatural bond," said the male voice. "Why is that not the case with these two?"

"Oh they're linked. But the divinity stones supersede their rapport."

It was the hunter speaking. Torie recognized the glee in her voice. They exchanged looks, each taking a deep breath to steel their resolve.

Back straight, chin up, they walked into the open, dimly lit space like they owned it.

"Well, hello everyone," said Torie, her voice strong and confident in the sudden silence. "Fancy seeing you here."

The two of them looked around, taking in the scene in a quick glance. The three men with guns were sitting on folding chairs around a small metal table. There were half-empty bottles of clear alcohol and plastic drinking cups scattered around, as well as a few makeshift cigarette ashtrays. The initial shock of seeing the two middle-aged women stroll into their midst wore off quickly, and they snatched up their guns and squared off, facing the women.

Torie swept her gaze across the open room and froze at what she saw in the center of the space.

Someone had created a makeshift fighting ring using heavy, yellow sand bags to create a confinement space of roughly twenty feet in circumference. There were pikes with iron chains attached, posted at either end of the ring. The chains were roughly fifteen feet in length, each with an iron, spiked collar at the end of them. The ring was coated in blood and fur, with long gouge marks at various intervals across the concrete surface.

Someone had been made to fight inside the circle, and Torie had a sinking feeling she knew who that someone was.

There was a raised platform at one end of the room where the hunter sat, cross-legged. When she saw the women approach, she frowned, giving Jasmin an especially dark look.

"How did you find me?" she asked.

"Wasn't that hard," said Jasmin. "You're not as clever as you think you are."

The hunter laughed and slipped down from the platform.

"No, I don't believe it was that easy. But whatever; it's all good."

Torie hated her cavalier attitude, and she felt her lips draw into a snarl, her voice harsher than she meant it to be. "What does that even mean? It's all good. How can any of this be good? Where are the werewolves you kidnapped?"

The men took a step forward in reaction to the threat in Torie's voice but stopped when the hunter raised a single hand.

"They, and that golem thing, are locked in the back. They provided us quite the entertainment earlier before we put them back in their cages. But I'm betting you know that already." She took a few steps closer, keeping an eye on Jasmin. "But what are ya'll doing here? You—" she pointed at Torie, " don't even have any power. Must have taken some guts for you to walk into this place."

She stopped and looked to her right at a sliding, steel barn door that was closed.

"Or are you after what's behind door number one? Did

you come to save your pet?" She stepped closer, moving deliberately to stand in front of Torie. "He must be a better lover than he is a fighter if you came all this way to rescue him. He must really have you dickmatized."

She laughed, and the men behind Torie and Jasmin roared at her not-funny joke.

Torie felt her anger collide with the feelings of helplessness she had endured for the past few weeks, and before she could stop herself, she slapped the hunter hard across the face. The sound of flesh smacking flesh silenced the room. Jasmin looked at her, eyes wide as she called up her magic and held it at the ready.

The hunter glared at Torie, clenching her fists at her sides. But then, as she noticed Torie shaking her hand and wincing in pain, she laughed uproariously.

"That literally hurt you more than it did me," she said. "Man, please don't ever let me get weak and old like the two of you."

She backed away, nodding at Torie. "I admire your spunk, old woman. Tell you what. You want your mutt back, go in there and get him." She stepped aside, sweeping her arm in a grand gesture towards the steel door behind her.

Torie didn't move, looking questioningly at Jasmin. That it was a trap of some kind was obvious. But if Elric was locked behind that door, she was willing to spring it.

"Torie, wait," said Jasmin, recognizing the look in her friend's eyes. "This wasn't the plan."

"Oh, so you did come in here with specific intentions?" said the hunter. "No matter. You won't be leaving."

Torie shrugged off Jasmin and rushed to the door. There was a latch that sprung free when she lifted it, allowing the door to be pushed open.

"Ah hell," said Jasmin, rushing to her friend's side. She

gave the hunter a hard look as she passed, moving quickly to stand by Torie's side at the entrance.

The light cast from flickering, overhead fluorescent bulbs added an extra hint of grit and seediness to the room. The air was putrid, a mix of years of cigarettes, poor ventilation, and sweat; all with a coppery undertone that Torie recognized as blood.

The hospital stretcher the golem rested on was in the middle of the floor. Beyond that were two steel cages; Max was in the one closest to them, and Elric sat in the one next to him.

"Elric!" Torie cried, racing across the room.

"Torie wait," said Jasmin, rushing after her. She stopped as she was passing the golem, remembering what her sister had said about Fionna.

The golem lay there, unmoving, his body strangely rigid. Jasmin reached out, patting his jacket gently.

"Fi...you in there? It's me, Jasmin."

There was a rustle of fabric and a flash of dark brown as the squirrel shifter leapt from the folds of the golem's jacket and scurried up Jasmin's arm to rest on her shoulder. Together, they made their way over to where Torie was looking at Max and Elric. She had knelt next to the cages and was holding onto the bars of Elric's.

The two werewolves were in their human form, each naked and battered. There were long gouges in their torsos and bite marks on limbs that were deep enough to show bone. Both were weary and unresponsive, their heads resting back against the bars, eyes closed.

"Oh my God," said Torie. "What have they done to you? Jasmin, can you open the doors?"

"I can try," she said, summoning a charge of magic to her hand.

Immediately, Fionna started to squeak and chatter noisily, jumping up and down on Jasmin's arm.

"Fionna, what are you doing?" asked Jasmin. "Can you shift back to human form so you can speak to us?"

Again, they were met with a chorus of chitters and screeches, but the shifter remained in her squirrel form. She vaulted off Jasmin's arm to land on top of the cage, chittering wildly at them.

"What is wrong with her?" asked Torie.

"No idea. It was your magic that allowed you to talk to them in animal form. I can't understand a word she's saying. Fionna, before the hunter sees you, get out of here...there's a window that's broken out up there—" she motioned to the rafters, "—see if you can get out. Opal is around back waiting for my magical signal. She has a plan to take the hunter out. Go wait with her until we can get these guys out of the line of fire."

Fionna screeched at the top of her lungs, looking from the caged wolves to Torie and Jasmin, gnashing her teeth together so hard, Torie was afraid they might break.

"What in the world?" Torie said.

But before she could say more, a slight moan escaped Elric's mouth as he opened his eyes and lifted his head slightly.

"Elric! Wake up, please. It's Torie. We've come to get you out of here."

The wolf looked over at her. One eye was black and nearly swollen shut, and the other was slow to focus on her.

"Torie?" he said, his voice as ragged and torn as his flesh. "Is that really you? You need to go. Get out of here while you can."

"I'm not leaving you. Jasmin is going to get these doors open and then we're getting you and Max out of here." She nodded to Jasmin, who raised her hand, pointing her palm at the door hinges.

"No, Jasmin, don't," said Max. He was now sitting up as well, his eyes focused on the blue magic that circled Jasmin's hand. "It's a trap, they knew you were coming."

"It's okay, Max," said Torie. "We have a little surprise of our own planned. Opal is waiting outside to—"

"No!" Elric barked. The effort caused him to spit blood and wince in pain. "She's…she's with them. She's the one behind this…"

Torie looked at Jasmin, saw the doubt tinged by unimaginable hurt in her friend's eyes.

"What are you talking about, Elric?" said Torie. "That can't be true."

There was a sudden, blinding flash as more overheads flared to life, bathing the room in brightness. A slow clap came from an area somewhere above them.

Torie looked up and could just make out shapes that appeared to be sitting on the top of bleacher-like rows of steps built into the concrete wall. As her eyes adjusted to the brightness of the light, she could make out the forms of the men from the other room, their long guns slung across their backs.

Beside them stood the hunter, clapping slowly. She stood, leaning over the steps to look down at them.

"Damn. She almost opened the doors. That would have been fun to watch, wouldn't it, Auntie?"

Next to her, Opal appeared, smiling down at them. She leaned into the hunter, resting her head on her shoulder.

"Well, Mom," said the hunter, "this is looking like it's going to be one hell of a family reunion."

Chapter Twenty-Two

Jasmin's magic flared and then died down as she stared at the two women looking down on them.

Slowly, she stood and took a couple steps toward them.

"Opal...what is going on here?"

Torie could hear the hurt and confusion in her friend's voice as she bent down next to the cage containing Elric. She was examining the locking mechanism that kept her from opening the door.

"Torie, don't," he said. "There is something, some kind of magic, that triggers our rage instinct when we are removed from the cages. I think it's linked to the divinity objects the hunter has. They've been making me and Max fight one another for their enjoyment. I don't want you to see me like that; and I don't want to hurt you."

Torie looked at him and, for the first time, noticed the collar he was still wearing. The gemstone that dangled from it glinted in the light. Glancing over at Max, she saw that he wore the same collar and stone. She opened her mouth to speak, but before she could, Elric cut her off.

"I've tried removing it. It's sealed with some kind of spell. You have to get out of here, forget about me."

"I'm not leaving you to die here, Elric, so you can forget about that happening."

He placed a hand against the bars, his fingers entwining with hers.

"She isn't going to kill us. She's turning us in for the money and our old boss is paying her well so that he has the luxury of killing us. But if I leave this cage, I can't control what I might do to you. I couldn't bear the thought…"

"Christ, the both of you," moaned Max. "If you don't stop whining, I'm going to save our old boss the pleasure and off myself. Elric is right; you and Jasmin get out of here. And take Fionna with you. She's starting to look like a Scooby snack to me."

The squirrel shifter hissed at the wolf and continued to scamper around the top of the crate.

"Why isn't she shifting to human?" Torie asked.

"She can't," Max said. "There is something here that seems to keep her trapped in her animal form; we were as well, until just a bit ago. Could be the contact she had with the golem, the mud he's made from short-circuited my brain, so who knows what it's doing to her. This whole place is crawling with dark magic. Spirit magic."

Torie knew he meant it was power generated by Opal. She turned her attention to Jasmin and walked over to stand with her. Jasmin had tears flowing down her cheeks and the set of her jaw told Torie she didn't trust herself enough to speak.

"Why are you doing this? Both of you," demanded Torie.

"Why do you think?" answered the hunter. "Revenge? Money? Hatred? All of the above, maybe?"

"For what?" asked Torie. "She hasn't even been in your life at all. And the two of you haven't spoken for the better part of two decades!" she yelled, addressing each of them. "Why would you show up now to do this?"

"Look at you," said Opal. "Standing up for her. And I'm sure were things reversed she would be there defending you as well. You know she thinks of you as her family."

Torie swallowed hard. "She *is* my family."

"Yeah, well we are her *actual* family; her *blood*," said the hunter. "And yet she walked away from us. Threw us out like so much trash. She destroyed my life, so it's only fitting that I get to destroy hers."

Torie shook her head in dismay. Her words were failing her and her mind raced, trying desperately to come up with something—anything—that could help them.

"Sharice," said Jasmin. Her voice was raw with emotion.

"I'm sorry, what did you say?" said the hunter.

"I said Sharice. It was the name I gave you. The last word I would whisper to myself at night before I fell asleep. I would say your name and pray that you were in a good place."

The hunter didn't speak. Instead, she glared at her mother, and Torie could almost feel the anger radiating off her in waves.

"How dare you," she said.

She leapt into the air and crashed to a landing, feet away from Jasmin and Torie. The two of them nearly tripped trying to backpedal away from her. Fists at her sides, she stalked to where they stood, standing inches from them.

"A good place, Jasmin? Really, that's what you wished for me? You never once considered that maybe a good place would have been with you? Someone who would love me and take care of me?" The menace in her voice grew with each question.

"Never once did I not love you," said Jasmin.

"Then wouldn't you think I should have been with the person that loved me the most?" said the hunter, her voice bitter and strained.

"Love is not the same as being able to take care of someone. Because I loved you, I did what I did. I had no idea what kind of life I would have and, at the time, I honestly did what I thought was best for you."

She turned away from the hunter and raised her face to her sister.

"And you. We knew one another. We are sisters."

"No," said Opal, "we *were* sisters. But you walked away from me. Made me feel so guilty for what happened to our mother. You never once apologized."

"I had nothing to apologize for. You ran away, Opal! If anything, I'm not the one that should be saying I'm sorry."

By now, Jasmin's face was wet with tears, and anger made her voice shake.

"You don't know what I've been through," said Opal. "What *we've* been through; your daughter and me. You cast us both out."

"Boo hoo," said Torie. "So you've had it rough when you were younger. Welcome to life. You think Jasmin's life was a waltz in the park?"

"Quiet," said the hunter, raising her hand to strike Torie.

"I would not do that," said Jasmin. Her voice was firm and her eyes flashed power that stopped the hunter in her tracks.

She lowered her arm and faced Jasmin.

"Again, you side against your own flesh and blood. You would choose a stranger over your own daughter."

"I would choose someone who has shown me time and time again that she has my back over someone who tried to stab it," Jasmin replied, turning to look once again at her sister. "How did this even happen? How did the two of you meet?"

"After a while, all of the foster families I was placed with kept returning me to the state, so I finally decided I was old enough to run off and take care of myself," started the hunter. She stopped when she saw the look on Jasmin's face. "What? You didn't know I was a ward of the state?"

"No, that's not possible. I left you with..."

"You dropped me outside a fire department."

"No, I read that you were placed with a loving family."

The hunter laughed. "Interesting thing happens when a loving family realizes their daughter is different. When I started showing an affinity for aggression and getting into fights at an early age, coupled with my emerging hunter's instincts and abilities; well, let's just say that a loving family will always choose the safety of their natural born children over a stray they picked up. You know what happens when a family dog bites one of the kids, right? Well, I was that dog. In every foster home I was placed in.

"Until I had enough and took off on my own. I don't know why, but I wanted to find my real family...family that, oh I don't know, maybe could tell me where I came from and what I was. All I had to go on was the locket you left me. One night, I beat up a police officer and made him run the picture of you through a nationwide database, looking for hits.

"It came back with Aunt Opal. The two of you looked

enough alike that she was a close match. I tracked her down in New Orleans…and the rest is history."

"Imagine my surprise at finding out I had a blood niece," said Opal. "One that looked so much like you when you were her age. I was even more surprised to find out she was a hunter. Do you know how rare those are?" She chuckled. "Of course you don't. But I did. Not only is she a hunter, but she will still grow into her magic one day. She is going to be something the world has never seen before.

"And to think, you should have been a part of that."

"But instead, I almost never was," said the hunter. "You don't know how many times I thought about taking my own life before I found Opal. I told her that. I told her everything. And you know what? She listened to me. She helped me to control the anger; to focus my rage. To harness my strength."

"And let me guess, she sold you out to the highest bidder. Turned you into a mercenary," said Jasmin.

"We weren't all fortunate enough to stumble into a town where witches prosper from old money," said Opal.

"And that's all you want, isn't it?" said Torie. "Money."

"Not just money," said Opal. "We intend to hurt someone who hurt us. Her more than me. She was your daughter, Jasmin. What you did to her shows me what you really think of family."

"You're both crazy and angry at the wrong person," said Torie. "You've focused on anger so long it's made you blind. Bad memories are designed to fade for a reason; but the two of you kept picking at them so they couldn't heal over. And look where it's brought you."

"You know, I am going to enjoy hurting you," said the hunter. "You think you're so much better than us, her flesh and blood." She reached inside her leather jacket and withdrew a gleaming silver blade. "I am going to deliver Max, alive, to my employer, but unfortunately, Elric tried to escape and, well, I had to put him down. But I'm sure my employer will be happy with one werewolf to skin."

She stepped close to Torie, searching the woman's eyes for signs of fear.

"Then I'm going to gut you, in front of Mommy Dearest, because I know how much that will hurt her."

"And me?" said Jasmin. "No special plans for me?"

"Oh, we are saving the best for last," said the hunter. "See, we are going to use you to raid all the money from the witch's trust fund here in Singing Falls. That money will set Aunt Opal and I up for life. And then, when I come into my power, I'm coming back to this little hell mouth wannabe, and things are going to change in a big way."

Jasmin laughed. "You know I'm not helping you do that. It will have to be over my dead body."

Now it was Opal who laughed. "Well, more like undead body. See, you forget. Spirits are my specialty. And Metrian here has been looking for a new physical body to take for a spin." At the mention of his name, the black spirit materialized next to Opal, winding his form around hers until he was glaring at them from behind her shoulder.

"Sounds like you have it all figured out," said Jasmin. "But you forgot one little thing."

"What's that, Mommy?" said the hunter, sarcasm dripping from her tongue.

"Torie isn't the only one who has my back."

Jasmin had been facing the hunter and her sister with her hands behind her back. As they spoke, her fingers wove a complex web of magic that had snaked along the floor behind her, making its way to the cages that held Max and

Elric. It climbed the front until it reached the sealed bolts that fastened and locked the doors.

With the flick of her finger, she commanded the bolts to release, opening the doors. As one, the two werewolves leapt from the cage, roaring their defiance.

Chapter Twenty-Three

The two men shifted to their full wolf form as they exited their cages. They howled in defiance as they moved in a blur. Jaws wide, fangs dripping with saliva, they leapt for everyone in sight.

Jasmin pushed Torie behind her and threw up a shield to protect them as Max pounced on the two of them, his claws throwing off sparks as they raked the blue barrier that protected the women. Jasmin concentrated, causing the barrier to pulse just enough to throw Max off them to crash into the base of the bleachers.

Elric paused, throwing back his head to emit a long, hellish howl that raised the hair on the back of Torie's neck. Then, he leapt at the hunter, catching her by surprise.

He shifted in mid-air, changing from wolf into his hybrid form. He landed a blow with his right fist across her head, temporarily stunning her. Rather than press his advantage, he grabbed her silver knife in his left hand and somersaulted backwards off her.

Smoke rose from the fist where he clenched the blade, and a disturbing sizzling sound could be heard throughout the space. He didn't wince or drop the weapon; instead, he turned and sprinted for the table where the golem lay.

"Stop him!" screamed Opal, realizing what his objective was.

The men raised their guns and began to squeeze off shots at the werewolf. One hit him in the leg, knocking him backward. He roared, rolling to regain his footing and continued towards the golem. Before another shot could be taken, Max had gained the lofted perch the gunmen claimed. With fang and claw, he set into them, ignoring their screams of terror.

Opal raised a hand and fired a bolt of white light at Elric. It struck him, only to glance off without slowing his progress. Her jaw dropped as she glanced at Jasmin. Her sister smiled, her eyes glowing with blue power.

The same power that glinted around Elric as Opal's magic had slid off him.

"She's shielding him!" Opal yelled to her niece. "Stop him now!"

The hunter made her way to her feet and started sprinting after Elric, her form barely recognizable as she crossed the space even quicker than he had. His head start was just enough to let him jump onto the stretcher and straddle the golem. He raised the knife above his head and plunged it downward, aiming for the golem's chest.

The tip of the blade never made contact, stopping inches from the creature's body.

The hunter had Elric's arm in her grasp and pitted her own strength against his, keeping her weapon from piercing the golem. With a heave and an exertion of strength that was beyond even Elric's, she threw the werewolf off the stretcher, ripping the blade away from him at the same time.

In a single, fluid motion, she scooped up the blade and leapt over the stretcher to land atop the wolf. She raised her blade and drove it downward. This time, there was no interference and the silver knife hissed as it cleaved through the werewolf's flesh, tearing bone and sinew.

Elric's roar was a soul-wrenching cross between a howl and a scream.

He slowly reached up, impotently clawing for the hunter's face. She shrugged his feeble gesture away and laughed as he slowly reverted to his human form. The long, silver blade made a disgusting, wet, sucking sound as she withdrew it from his chest and turned her attention to Jasmin and Torie.

Torie dropped to her knees and screamed, her eyes focused on the bloody form of her lover. She didn't notice the hunter as she walked up to them and slowly pushed her blade into the glowing barrier that protected her and Jasmin. The point of the blade hissed as it made contact with Jasmin's magic; and ever so slowly, it began to penetrate the shield.

Jasmin grunted, shifting her focus to stop the attack. She pulled the barrier away from them, concentrating it into a single shield that separated her from the hunter's knife.

Opal saw her opening and raised both hands, her eyes growing white as her lips moved soundlessly; invoking an ancient enchantment that only the spirits could hear.

Responding to its mistress's commands, the wraithlike form of Metrian slithered down the wall and settled into the still unmoving form of the golem.

The mud creature flexed in response, before slowing rising and stepping off the stretcher.

Torie was numb. She felt like the breath had been knocked out of her and tears blurred her vision. The sudden grip around the back of her neck was so tight that she could not even let out a gasp as the golem lifted her into the air.

"Torie!" screamed Jasmin. She attempted to turn to help her friend but instantly felt the hunter's blade progress deeper into her shield. She concentrated, redoubling her efforts to keep the knife from reaching her.

She nearly buckled under the tremendous power of the hunter as beads of sweat broke out across her forehead. She knew it was only a matter of time before the hunter broke through. As her mind raced for solutions, a small blur at her feet raced across the floor.

Fionna leapt onto the hunter's legs and scrambled up her body at dizzying speed. Biting, scratching, and clawing at every inch of the hunter's body, until she reached her head. There, Fionna dug her claws into the hunter's afro puffs, biting savagely into her scalp and face.

The hunter screamed, dropping the knife and grabbing at her own head, trying in vain to grasp the squirrel shifter.

Jasmin took advantage of the distraction to unleash a bolt of magic into her daughter, slamming her across the space to crash heavily onto the floor. Fionna was a blur as tiny sprays of blood flew into the air where she made contact with the hunter's face.

Immediately Jasmin turned to look for Torie.

The golem held her high above his head in a one-handed choke. Torie held onto his arm, flailing like a rag doll as she tried hopelessly to break free.

Jasmin attacked, using the full force of her magic against the creature, but to no avail. The sizzling bolt that struck him glanced off, slicing to the side. She stepped closer, raising her hand to attack again; this time, the golem stammered under her attack, but did not relinquish his grip on Torie's neck.

Jasmin launched herself at her foe, landing on his back as she tried to physically tear him free from Torie. She could see Torie starting to struggle less, her eyes becoming cloudy as her body jerked spasmodically.

Jasmin cried out, calling for anyone to help her as she struggled against a man made of clay that was about to kill her best friend.

Her voice sounded far away to Torie's ears, and it was fading fast. Her vision was foggy; silver lights began to flash in her periphery, and she felt herself losing consciousness.

This was it; at least the golem hadn't snapped her neck. While that would have been fast and painless, it would not have let her get one last blurry look at someone who had grown to mean so much to her. It wouldn't have let the happy memories of her time in Singing Falls play out in her mind.

She felt herself slump in the golem's grip.

Her last memories began to fade; her mother's house, fresh baked scones at Jim's Bakery, fresh morning coffee.

Nights in Elric's arms.

Her son, that she would not get to see become the man he was meant to be.

Shawn. Her son.

The thought sparked something in her. Something that wasn't quite ready to disappear out of the world just yet. She began to struggle again, only this time she felt something. Something in her pocket burning to be free.

She reached down and felt something small and hard.

It was the white gem Jasmin had given her days ago.

Her arm felt as heavy as lead as she forced herself to dig

into her jeans and fish it out. She acted out of instinct, reaching up and slamming it into the golem's forehead.

There was a flash of white as pure magic blasted into the creature, making him drop her to the ground as it clasped both hands to its torn forehead, staggering backwards.

But Torie wasn't finished.

She held the gem in her fist, feeling the power it contained. The magic flowed into her and deep in the recesses of her soul, she recognized its touch.

The gem flared again, this time her own long-dormant power flowing into it to mix with the latent energy contained within. She struck out, plunging her fist into the golem, tearing a black hole in him. She felt the divinity object that was buried within his side and grabbed it, holding both it and the white gem in her fist.

Her eyes flared with power as she poured her will into the two stones. They ignited and erupted from within, tearing through the golem and burning his body to cinder.

Metrian shrieked in agony as he sought to flee the crumbling body, but Torie had plans for the spirit that didn't include escape. She formed a red orb around the smoky creature, trapping it within. Then, her mouth moving slowly, she called on her power to burn the creature, purging it from the world of man and sending its tattered remains back to the dark ether from which it had escaped.

Opal's scream reached their ears, and Torie saw her floating down towards them, carried by ghostly tentacles, her face a mix of fear and anger. Instead of attacking them, she ran past them, kneeling at the side of the hunter, gathering up her bloody form in her arms as she cried.

Away from her, Fionna sat, back in her human form, and stared in horror at what she had done to the hunter.

From where they sat, Torie could not tell if the hunter was breathing as Opal rocked her limp form back and forth.

She got up and ran to Elric's side.

The wolf was covered in blood, and spreading from the wound in his chest was a patchwork of black spiderwebs that seemed to be spreading under his skin, traveling across his body.

He wasn't breathing, and if his heart was beating it was too shallow for Torie's fingers to pick up as she felt the side of his neck.

She looked up just in time to see Max arrive at her side, bloody from his fight with the gunmen. Jasmin dropped down beside her as well, placing a hand on Torie's shoulder.

"Torie, help him," she said, her voice shaking.

"What...how?"

"The same way you saved your life. Save his. They're your magics. Call to them."

Torie looked down at the man she loved. He was so still, so fragile in her arms. She placed her palm on his chest and leaned in until her lips were mere inches from his.

Then, closing her eyes, she whispered.

> *"Light of my life, depth of my heart,*
> *I pray it is not yet time for us to part.*
> *Grant me the will to take your pain,*
> *as I purge this blackness from your veins."*

Elric's body stiffened in her arms as he began to convulse. The black ichor that seemed to be coursing through his body gathered itself and raced up his torso, into his neck, and then flowed out through his parted lips, entering Torie's mouth.

She jumped back, gasping for breath as she clawed at

her throat. Panic set in, and her eyes grew wide as she looked around for help.

"Torie," said Jasmin, calmly, reaching for her friend's hand. "You got this. Focus your mind and do what you have to do."

Despite the fear, Torie did as she was told. She calmed herself, sank within her emotions, and touched something that she had given up hope of ever finding.

Her magic.

Her hex power, buried and apart from her for so long, now sang.

She called to it, embraced it, felt it burn through her, blasting away the black poison she had absorbed from Elric. It blasted out of her, pouring out of every pore in her body as radiant white light; the blackness burned away by the power she drew upon.

When the last of it had left her system, she stood there; strong, fierce, and complete.

Her eyes glowed white, and a patch of silver streaked through the center of her hair, from front to back. She felt better than she had in months and her tears flowed freely as gratitude washed over her.

She took Jasmin's hand again and together they turned to face her sister.

Opal, still cradling the body of the hunter, glared at them, her eyes burning with hatred.

Torie reached out with her magic, brushing it over the hunter.

"There is still the spark of life in her, Opal," she said. "Let us help her."

"Please," said Jasmin, holding her hand out to her sister.

Opal spat her rage at them. "Never. I will never let you

touch her. She would rather be dead than know you saved her."

With that, she cast her gaze to the ceiling, eyes white as she called on spirits to take them away.

Before either of the witches could stop her, sister and niece were gone in a blinding nimbus of light and smoke.

Chapter Twenty-Four

"You sure about this?" Jasmin asked.

Torie nodded. "It's time."

"It's going to be a lot of work; and money," added Fionna.

The three of them stood at the end of a gravel road, looking out over an idyllic meadow. It was bordered by trees on all sides with the only break being the one to allow the patch of gravel where they were standing.

"I just don't see why you want to build when you can just stay with me," said Jasmin. "I have plenty of room."

"And you also have a life of your own that you need to get on with. We both do," replied Torie. "Plus, my mother's house was pretty much totaled. It would cost as much to rebuild it as it would to build new. Besides, that was her home. It's time I made one of my own."

She wanted to add that it would be the first time she had ever done that; created a house that was all hers. Not her parents'. Not her ex-husband's.

"It's just…I was getting used to having you around all the time," said Jasmin.

"You mean you were used to my morning breakfasts."

"Well, I know I was used to that," said Fionna. "Now what will I do? Who will I drop in on that has perfect coffee, perfect crisp bacon, and perfect blueberry scones?"

"It's like it's the end of an era," said Jasmin sadly.

The three of them turned and walked across the driveway and onto a small path that broke through the trees. The morning light greeted them as the exited the wooded patch to a cobble stone path that led to the side entrance to Jasmin's house.

"I'll literally be two minutes away from you," said Torie. "I'm pretty sure you can still come over for breakfast anytime you want. You too, Fionna," she added before the squirrel shifter could lodge a complaint.

"Well, with my knees you might as well be miles away," said Jasmin, feigning insult.

"Please. I saw the way you jumped on that golem's back," said Fionna. "Them knees were just fine."

"*Were* is the operative word," said Jasmin. "I have permanent aches settling in from that. I'm sticking to magic from now on. You shifters can have all that physical nonsense."

They all laughed as they made their way into the kitchen.

"So, how are you?" asked Torie. "We haven't really talked much about what happened that night."

Jasmin shrugged. "Well, I guess I'm doing fine. I mean, for someone whose only sister teamed up with her long-lost daughter to try and kill her; I'm right as rain."

The sarcasm was tinged with hurt, and Torie smiled at her friend.

"I still can't believe Opal orchestrated all of that," said Torie. "When you called her asking for help because I had lost my power, she seized on the opportunity to take her revenge on you for all these imagined slights against her. And she dragged your daughter into it as well."

"Looks that way," said Jasmin. "Elric and Max paid their old boss in Trinity Cove a visit and settled with them once and for all. In exchange, they got some intel on my daughter and Opal. They saw the chance to use Elric and Max's old mob bosses by promising them she'd bring the wolves back to them for a hefty fee. That gave them a cover for wanting to come to town in the first place. She had been stalking me for years apparently. She knew everything that was going on in my life. Knew what it would take to hurt me the deepest."

"So there was never really a hit put out on Max and Elric?" asked Torie.

"No. But of course, she made the bosses an offer they couldn't refuse. An eye for an eye, so to speak."

"So no word on Opal or your daughter? Where they might have gone?"

Jasmin shook her head, her eyes cold as she stared straight ahead.

"Do you think we'll see them again?" pressed Fionna.

"I'd bet on it. Maybe not tomorrow, or the next day. Probably not anytime soon. But one day, I'm betting they turn up again," said Jasmin.

"Like a bad penny," said Fionna.

"Or herpes," grumbled Jasmin.

"Maybe we should look for them," said Torie. "I mean, it's your family; you could try getting through to them again."

Jasmin shook her head and placed both arms around Fionna and Torie.

"This," she shook them gently, "is my family."

Torie could only smile as she pulled away from the two of them. The last thing she wanted was to start crying first thing in the morning.

"So, what about you," said Fionna. "How are the boys?"

Torie sighed. "They're good. Max is back in his role as sheriff so, things in town are getting back to normal."

"I hope he replaces those deputies of his. He was missing for three days and not one of them went looking for him. Lazy-ass shifters. No offense, Fionna."

"None taken," she replied cheerily.

"And what about Elric?" asked Jasmin.

Torie couldn't hold back her smile. "He's as great as ever. Things are really good with us."

"You know, he is welcome to sleep over," said Jasmin. "I can magically soundproof all the rooms so you too can get your freak on if that worries you."

Torie blushed and gave her friend a cross look. "That won't be necessary, Jasmin. We are just fine."

"Uh huh. If you say so," Jasmin said.

"I hear the humans in town are pissed that their magical abilities all went away," said Fionna. "I feel sorry for Myra Simms."

Jasmin nodded. "Yes. Her grief over the death of her husband was so great that she used a stone to animate mud. That's some powerful magic, by the way." She glanced at Torie. "Even Opal was impressed by that. I kind of think that was what she wanted the golem for…to reverse engineer how your magic was able to create it. Good thing you destroyed it."

Torie didn't answer but instead began rummaging through the refrigerator.

"And Fionna, it was never *their* magic," said Jasmin. "The crystals they found that had absorbed Torie's magic would have eventually run out of juice, even if Torie had not reacquired said magic."

"How did you get it back, Torie?" asked Fionna.

"I'm not sure. I guess it was always there, and being placed in a position where I was afraid for my life allowed me to tap into it."

Jasmin shook her head. "No, sis, that ain't it. You were in a position where you were afraid for someone else's life that you valued more than your own. You were fighting for something, someone, that you loved more than yourself. That's growth. And that's what allowed you to tap back into your hex."

"Well, one thing is for certain," Torie said. "I will never take my powers for granted. I feel whole once again, and I am so thankful for that."

She took a pitcher of fresh orange juice out and sat it on the island, followed by a chilled bottle of champagne. Looking across the kitchen to a glass-fronted cabinet, she saw the last thing she needed. She concentrated, and with a nod, summoned a trio of champagne flutes from the cabinet to her hands.

"Morning Mimosas," said Jasmin. "Perfect."

"When I lived in New York, I learned the perfect Mimosa recipe," she said. It felt odd, referencing her life before Singing Falls. It seemed so far away that it barely registered in her memory.

She poured champagne into the flutes, held the orange juice carafe next to them and gently waved her hand between them.

"The secret is to only provide a whiff of orange scent into the champagne. No more; no less."

Jasmin and Fionna laughed uproariously at the image before each taking a glass. The three women clinked glasses, making a point to stare one another in the eyes as they did so.

"To friendship," said Torie. "Long may it reign."

"And to having each other's back," said Jasmin. "I wouldn't be here without you two. I love you ladies."

"And we love you," said Fionna. "So, Torie, this house you're building next door; what's the details on it? How many bedrooms? What kind of kitchen are you going to have? Oh! Are you going to put in a panic room?"

"More importantly, will Elric be moving in?" asked Jasmin.

Torie laughed. "No, he will not be moving in. At least not at first."

Jasmin and Fionna laughed and began chatting about decor, wall color and the best time to go furniture shopping. Torie sipped her champagne and watched them with affection.

She had come a long way and was grateful to the two women standing before her that had been an integral part of her life. She didn't know what was coming next, but she knew that with friends like these, there was nothing they would not be able to handle.

vinci-books.com/hexchocolate

Murder in a magical town?

Witch Torie Bliss must uncover the truth before chaos reigns. With
secrets swirling and danger rising, can she save Singing Falls and
the people she loves?

Turn the page for a free preview…

Hex and Chocolate: Chapter One

"Okay. Last chance to back out. Are you sure you want to do this?" Elric's voice was low and gravelly in Torie's ear. She felt her body tense in response.

"Yes. I think I'm ready for it." She had no idea if this was something she would be able to do or not, but her instincts told her it was time.

"You know I don't want to hurt you," Elric said. He moved closer behind her, pushing up against her, each exhale of his breath moved the hair on the back of her neck.

"We've been dancing around this long enough. It's time to see if I can do it. And don't hold back. I'm a lot tougher than I look."

"Relax, don't stiffen up. If you're tense, your body won't move the way it needs to in order to make this work. Don't hold your breath."

Torie nodded and took a deep breath in through her nose, and exhaled slowly, willing the tension in her body to flow out with her breathing.

Then, it happened so fast, she felt panic flood her system as Elric shifted to his hybrid werewolf form and threw his weight onto her.

She let out a sharp grunt as she heard him growl into her ear. His hard, muscular arms closed around her as he grabbed her from behind, pinning her arms to her side.

Torie willed herself to remain calm and trusted her body to respond appropriately. Lifting one foot off the ground, she drove her heel into Elric's instep, while simultaneously snapping her head back, crashing it into his face.

He howled in pain and loosened his grasp on her, just enough for her to raise one fist before slamming it down and back, connecting with his groin. This caused the wolf to break his grip and allowed her to turn and face him. Without thinking, she thrust her hand into his windpipe and then the struck the bridge of his nose with the heel of her hand.

The wolf staggered back, grasping his snout and gasping for air.

Torie retreated, her hands covering her mouth.

"Oh my God...Elric! Are you okay? I swear I didn't mean to lash out that hard." She stepped forward, putting her arm around the wolf as he gasped for breath and shifted back into his human form.

"I'm alright," he said, reassuring her with a smile. "Good thing wolves heal a lot faster than humans." He stood up straight, showing her his nose. The bleeding had stopped almost immediately, and he was no longer gasping for breath. "That was excellent."

Despite her fear that she had hurt him, Torie smiled.

"That kind of felt good," she said. "The adrenaline rush was something I wasn't ready for. But still, are you sure you're okay?" She looked down at his midsection.

"Yeah. That was a stinger, but you need to get used to striking out full strength. So there's no other way to do this."

"Maybe you should wear one of those padded suits... like they do in the women's self-defense class ads I see at the YMCA."

Elric shook his head. "It's not the same. I need to feel what you're dishing out, to make sure you're striking the right way, with the right force to immobilize someone if need be. Besides, believe me when I say; you can't hurt me. Unless you use magic, of course."

Torie smiled, rubbing at a kink in her neck that radiated small twinges of pain into her shoulder. "But I learned a lot about myself when I lost my powers. First, that I can't always depend on them for protection. I need to learn how to handle myself in a crunch. And second, I need to get in better shape. You teaching me self-defense accomplishes both of those things."

Elric moved to stand in front of her. His tall, muscular frame dwarfing her.

"Well, you're doing a great job." He took her hand in his and raised it to the center of his forehead. "Just remember. The most delicate parts of a man, the weakest parts, all run down the center of his body. The eyes, the bridge of the nose, the windpipe, the solar plexus, and of course, the groin." As he named each part, he trailed her hand down the center of his body.

Torie blushed at the last delicate bit. But, in truth, it was more from excitement than embarrassment.

"The hell kind of self-defense is this?" said a voice from behind them.

Torie spun around to see her friend Jasmin standing at the door, hands on her hips.

"Hello, Jasmin. Come on in; it's not what it looks like," Torie said.

"Uh huh. I'm sure. Well at least now I know why you still haven't gotten any furniture. Y'all need a lot of space for all that…defense that's going on."

Elric laughed and moved to a corner of the large living room to retrieve a duffel bag that had been tossed there, along with his shoes.

"No, I don't have furniture yet because I need to experience the space a little more to decide how I want to decorate," said Torie.

Her new home had completed construction just under a month ago. It was a beautiful, traditional two-story with a grand center hall, double staircase that led to the upper level. The house had two separate wings that were angled back slightly from the center portion, offering her a towering, two-story master suite on one side, and spacious guest accommodations along with a study, theater room, library, and a second den in the other wing.

The main hall was dominated by a great room that opened into a massive kitchen with a wall of windows that looked out over Torie's spacious green house and impressive old growth woods beyond that. The upper level balcony contained a loft area with two more bedrooms, each with their own en suite.

It was a grand home, and certainly more space than Torie would ever need.

"I love this house, Torie," Jasmin said. "But are you sure you want to open it up to just any old Tom, Dick or Harry that wanders through?"

"It's not going to be an open house," said Torie. "I just feel incredibly blessed, and I want to give back to this wonderful community that has opened its doors to me, by doing the same. I want everyone to know that if they are ever in a jam, they have a place to stay if need be. Besides, this place is about the same size as yours, and you live alone."

"Hey, don't compare yourself to me. As Madonna said, I am a material girl. I live for luxury. I just figured after everything you went through, and the life you left in New York, you wouldn't go for something like this again."

Torie smiled weakly. "You're right. Honestly, I loved the house my mother lived in, the one I stayed in when first moving here. Part of me wanted to just rebuild it after it was destroyed in that brawl with your daughter...er, I mean, that hunter...but I couldn't. That home belonged to my mother, so I decided I needed to create something that is uniquely mine. I want it to be filled with all the things that are important to me, and what's most important to me is family and friends.

"I want Shawn to feel like he can come here and stay for as long as he wants and not feel cramped. He can bring his friends, maybe at some point a wife and kids. Or a husband; whatever he wants. I want to create something that I can pass on to him and the generation after him."

"And what about a certain werewolf?" asked Jasmin, lowering her voice. "And maybe a houseful of pups?"

Torie mock slapped at her friend's arm. "Jasmin! Stop that. I am way past child-bearing age...so you know that is not happening."

"Oh, I'm just teasing," Jasmin said, laughing. "But seriously, the two of you look very happy. When are you going to make it official?"

Torie blushed slightly. "You never know. Maybe we have plans to go look at furniture this weekend. Together."

Jasmin stared at her friend, a mischievous smile breaking out on her face.

"Girl, you need to tell me everything. But first, you need to go change and meet me at my place so we can head into town to meet Fionna for coffee. She says she has news to share."

Torie checked her watch and nodded. If she hurried, she would just have time to shower and change.

"Elric, I'm going to head into town with Jasmin. Can you lock up?"

"Not a problem," the wolf replied. "I'll see you tonight for dinner. I have a surprise for you."

Torie smiled and blew him a kiss as she walked Jasmin to the door.

"What was that about?" Jasmin wanted to know.

"I don't know. But I can't wait to find out," Torie replied.

Thirty minutes later they were heading into town in Jasmin's blue SUV. The gentle kaleidoscope created by the sunlight breaking in and out of the large trees lining the winding road from the small enclave of houses where Jasmin and Torie lived was mesmerizing.

"You know, I tease you a lot, but Elric is a good man. You lucked out with him," said Jasmin.

"I know. And he is so patient with me. I couldn't ask for more."

"Well, you could ask for a fat ring. Make it official and all."

Torie laughed. "You know, I'm not sure I want to get married again. In the long run, it doesn't mean anything really. If anything, it adds another layer of complication to a good situation; things are going really good with us now."

"Yes, and the enemy of good is better. Still, I'm happy for the both of you. But that doesn't mean I will stop teasing him every chance I get."

"And what about you, Missie? When are you climbing back on that relationship horse? As long as I've known you now, I don't think I've seen you interested in anyone."

"We aren't talking about me. And if we were talking about me, I'd tell you not to go worrying about me. Trust me, my needs are met."

Torie shifted her weight so that she was facing Jasmin.

"So, are you admitting that you're dating someone?"

"Easy there, Nancy Drew. I am a grown woman and what you call 'dating' we grown women call getting ours when we want it."

Torie looked at her appreciatively.

"You know, I love your attitude. You always know what you want and don't bother conforming to what society tells women of our age we should be doing."

Jasmin laughed.

"What society wants is for us to quietly disappear after we turn forty. In some members of society's mind, we are better off unheard and unseen. But you know what? I'm just hitting my stride. I feel better than I did at twenty-five, in mind, spirit and body. Especially body. I know what I like, and I'll tell you a little secret; men like that I tell them what I need. Nobody has time for all that fumbling around and training; I know all the spots they need to hit on my body and in what order."

Torie couldn't help but laugh. "You sound like a teacher."

"Nope. This ride is only for the experienced. I might

take them up a notch, and they just need to hope they can hang. As the sign in my bedroom says, ride at your own risk."

Torie looked shocked. "You do not have that in your bedroom."

Jasmin smiled mischievously. "Okay, maybe not. But I'm thinking about it."

They rounded a curve and saw it at the same time.

A dark sedan had slid off the road, the front end was angled down into a ditch while the rear tires were perched on the dirt edge of the road. The brake lights were glowing red, but the car itself seemed to have stopped running.

Jasmin eased her SUV to a stop behind it, and they both jumped out.

Carefully, Torie made her way down into the ditch to stand beside the passenger door. A man slumped forward, his body resting against the steering wheel.

"Mister! Are you okay?" Torie rapped on the window to get his attention. When he didn't answer, she grasped the door handle and gave it a tug. The door opened and she reached in, gently nudging the man. Still he didn't respond, so she applied a little more pressure and eased him off the steering wheel and back into a sitting position. His head lagged to one side, and it was obvious, even before she laid two fingers on his neck, that the man was dead.

Jasmin gasped, placing a hand over her mouth when she leaned in and saw the man.

"What? Do you know him?" said Torie.

"That's Terry Blatt. He's the town mayor."

Hex and Chocolate: Chapter Two

Torie had her phone out and was beginning to dial when Jasmin waved a hand at her.

"Who are you calling?"

"I'm calling 9-1-1. We need an ambulance up here. Then I'm calling Max," Torie said.

"No, call Max first. Give him a head start and then call 9-1-1. I mean, he's definitely dead, so there's nothing an ambulance can do for him."

Torie hesitated but then ended her call and dialed the number for their friend and Sheriff instead. She spoke briefly into the phone and then hung up and placed her 9-1-1 call.

"Okay, everyone has been notified."

Torie watched as Jasmin opened the passenger side door and half entered the car. Then, closing her eyes, she waved her hand inside the car, her lips moving soundlessly. When she was finished, she stood up and looked at Torie.

"Anything?"

Jasmin shook her head. "Nothing. No magical residue,

and I also didn't pick up the latent presence of anyone else in the car with him. He was alone."

"You mean, he just pulled off the side of the road and died? Does that happen to people?"

Jasmin shrugged her shoulders, staring at the dead man before them.

"Maybe he had a heart attack or a stroke?"

Torie assessed the man as best she could. He seemed young and fit to her, and while it was difficult to gauge his height while in the position he was, he appeared to be around five feet ten inches and just under one hundred and seventy pounds.

"Is he even forty?" she asked.

"Unlikely. No one wants the job of mayor in this town, and he pretty much ran unopposed the last two election cycles. He was doing a great job from what I've heard."

Now it was Torie's turn to close her eyes as she reached out with her magic to probe the dead man in front of her. She fought the natural urge to recoil from his lifeless form as her magic snaked in and around the body. She withdrew her power, stepping back from the body.

"I don't sense anything out of the ordinary about the body. He's definitely human, and there are no signs that he died of anything mystical."

"Well, that's good. Cause around here, you never know anymore."

The blare of a siren interrupted them as a black Chevy Tahoe with the letter SFPD Sheriff stenciled on the side in white pulled up. Torie waved as Max stepped out, his gold sheriff's badge glistening in the sunlight.

"Hey, Torie. Jasmin. What have we got here?" he asked, circling the car.

"It's the mayor," said Jasmin. "We were headed into town and came across this."

Max studied the scene, his head swiveling from the car to the road and back again.

"Have you touched anything?" he asked.

Torie and Jasmin exchanged looks.

"Well, I mean...you know, we didn't know he was dead and thought we could help out, so we might have touched the body. But only a little. And once we realized he was dead we haven't messed with him since," said Torie.

Max nodded, noting her nervousness.

"Relax. I just need to make a note of that so we can rule out any DNA you might have transferred."

The two witches watched as he took out his notebook, scribbled something illegible and then resumed his inspection of the car. Putting on gloves, he opened the door and stuck his head inside. Torie could hear him inhaling deeply a few times before he walked back to where she and Jasmin were standing.

"Looks like he's had a few different people in the car with him, but nobody in the last day or so," he said. "Did either of you...er, sense anything odd?"

"If you're asking if he was killed by magic or a supernatural, no," said Jasmin.

Max cocked his head to one side, listening to something they could not hear.

"Ambulance is coming," he said. "You should probably be on your way. I'll let you know if we find anything out of the ordinary."

Torie nodded, just as the wail of the ambulance siren made its way to their less sensitive ears.

"This will be big news in town," said Jasmin. "We'll be around."

"I know you will," Max said as they made their way to Jasmin's SUV and pulled away just as the ambulance came to a screeching halt at the scene.

"What a shame," said Jasmin, shaking her head as they continued down the mountain.

"Did he have family?" asked Torie.

"I don't really know. It wasn't like we were friends or anything. He put in appearances, and was well liked, but at the same time was a loner. Come to think of it, I don't know anything about him that you couldn't find out on his website."

"But he's human, right? And he knew about the sub-community in Singing Falls?"

Jasmin nodded. "He was an ally. He believed in maintaining a peaceful co-existence between the humans and supernaturals. His voice will be missed."

They made the rest of the trip in silence, each sad at the loss of someone they really didn't know.

Fionna was saving them seats at Jim's Bakery, two saucers with cranberry and blueberry scones sat on the small coffee table surrounded by three leather chairs. Torie took a deep breath, inhaling the scent of flour, fresh baked bread, and sweetness of all kinds that always permeated the interior of the bakery.

"Oh, you guys," Fionna said as they approached. "I got your text. Are you okay?" She gave each of them a hug.

"We're alright," said Jasmin. "Better than the mayor, that's for sure."

"So did Max have any idea what happened?"

"None at all," said Torie. "It was really strange." She looked around, setting her purse in her chair. "I'm going to grab a coffee. Jasmin, can I get you one? Another for you, Fionna? Sorry about you having to wait so long for us."

"No, don't even think about it. And I'm fine, thanks."

"I'll have one of whatever you're having," said Jasmin.

A quick trip to the counter and Torie was back, catching the end of Jasmin's remark to Fionna.

"Really, Fionna, I don't think that is what the town is going to be focused on right now."

"Why not? I'm sure I won't be the first one to think about it."

"What are we thinking about?" asked Torie, setting the two cups of espresso down.

"Fionna is worried about the First Eve Festival and if it will still be held," said Jasmin.

"What's that?"

They both stared at her before Fionna's eyes grew as wide as her smile.

"That's right. You've never been here for First Eve! It's a weeklong festival that the town throws every year. It's great; all the shops on main street decorate their storefronts and stay open late to offer samples of their wares. Main Street gets blocked off for sidewalk artists to set up booths as well. There's candy, games, food...so much food! But the best thing of all has to be the chocolate contest."

Torie eyed her suspiciously as the squirrel shifter's eyes rolled back in her head. "I'll have to take your word for it." She laughed happily as she took a sip of her coffee.

"No, seriously, it's the best. You think the sweets here at Jim's are tasty, just wait till you try the ones at the festival. The chocolate competition is open to anyone who wants to enter. You should enter since—" She stopped, glancing at Jasmin.

"Since what?" Torie asked.

Fionna squirmed but didn't answer. Torie looked at Jasmin, arching her eyebrows.

"Well, the winner from the previous year not only gets the best table—front and center—at the contest, but they also get to be the official opener of the festival, along with the mayor."

"Okay," said Torie, "still don't see why I should enter."

"Well, your mother won last year. So you would be continuing the tradition. It's kind of a big honor," said Jasmin.

Torie didn't say anything as she sipped her espresso. She could sense Jasmin giving Fionna a disapproving look and quickly smiled at her friends.

"It's okay," she said. "It's nice knowing that my mother was such a bastion of the community here. I just hope that one day I can live up to her reputation. But I don't think creating chocolate confections will be how I do it." She noticed that Fionna still wasn't looking at her, so she reached over and placed a hand on her friend's knee. "Hey, really. I'm okay. But tell me, why is it called the First Eve celebration? What is the meaning behind it?"

"Well," said Fionna, perking up, "officially, it's the anniversary of the town's founding, when it was established way back in the days of yore."

"Days of yore? Really?" said Jasmin. "You know that was only a little over a hundred years ago, right? I mean, there are shifters in town who probably remember that night. You make it sound like it was a millennia ago."

"Whatever. That's the official reason."

Torie could tell by the way she said it that she was waiting to be asked more.

"And the unofficial reason?"

Fionna's eyes glittered and she leaned in close to the other two women.

"It's the night that a human male and his pregnant wife

were traveling through the area and became lost in a storm. They wandered into the woods and would have died if not for a family of fox shifters who took pity on them. They approached the family in human form and led them to shelter, bringing them food and water. The woman was too weak to continue the trek north, so the shifters suggested they stay with them, just until she was strong enough to continue.

"Then, they insisted she stay until the baby arrived. And by that point, the humans felt like they had found a new home and new friends. There was no need to move on.

"One by one, more human families moved into the little settlement, as well as more shifters. That's how Singing Falls got its start as a tolerance-based community. We accept everyone and believe that everyone deserves a second chance." She glanced at Jasmin, smiling.

Torie wasn't sure what that was about but pretended like she didn't see it.

"Well, that's all very interesting," she said, "but I don't think I'll be entering the contest."

"If there even is one," replied Fionna. "The mayor is the key figure and judge in the celebration. Without him, I wonder if the town will even hold the festival."

Torie didn't say anything as she resumed sipping her drink. Then her eyes widened as she remembered something.

"Fionna, what was it that you had to tell us? You said you had news you wanted to share."

"Yes, what was it that had you all worked up?" asked Jasmin.

Fionna had a sheepish look on her face.

"It seems so silly now. Especially in light of what just happened with the mayor," she said.

"Oh nonsense," said Jasmin. "Go ahead. Tell us."

Fionna pursed her lips then leaned in, eyebrows arched, like she was about to divulge the greatest secret in existence.

"Okay. I'm going to be having a birthday party!"

She delivered the news and sat back quickly into her chair, hands clasped together in excitement.

Torie blinked. "That's it? You're having a birthday party?"

Before she could continue, Jasmin was on her feet, wringing her hands in amazement as her face lit up in delight. She grabbed Fionna and gave her an enthusiastic hug.

"Girl, yes! I am so happy for you!"

Torie was all for birthday celebrations, but something about this seemed a little off from what she was used to.

"Am I missing something?" she asked.

Jasmin beamed, her smile lighting up the coffee shop. "She is celebrating her birthday! Do you know how big this is?"

Fionna rolled her eyes. "Of course she doesn't. How could she know?" They both sat down and stared at Torie before Fionna continued. "Shifters don't have birthdays. That's a human tradition."

Torie was genuinely confused at this point. "What do you mean you don't have a birthday? Everyone has a birthday."

"Technically, yes. Obviously, I know that I was born. But I don't know what day. It isn't something that a shifter celebrates because there is no meaning tied to it for us."

"So, if you don't celebrate your birthday, or know when it is, how do you know how old you are?" asked Torie.

Fionna shrugged. "I have no idea how old I am."

"And why have you chosen to adopt this human tradition now?" asked Jasmin.

"It was Glen's idea. She is really keen on me having a special day dedicated just to me. She has asked me to consider it for years, and now, lately, I've decided why not? Each year I am with her I'm reminded that, while we aren't promised forever, I can't imagine a future without her. So, if making me celebrate the passing of another year successfully makes her happy, then it makes me happy too."

Jasmin clapped her hands wildly. "I am so happy to hear that. Of course, it could also mean that you're taking one more step towards embracing life with humans a little more."

"Well, considering I'm practically married to one, I don't see how it could hurt. But anyway, that was my news. Kind of pales in comparison to what you guys just experienced."

"Well, a dead mayor does not take precedence over a best friend's first birthday!" said Jasmin. "We are throwing you a birthday party. When have you decided your birthday will be?"

"Two Saturdays from tomorrow. It will be the day before the kickoff to the Festival."

"This will be so much fun," said Jasmin. "You leave everything to us. You just show up and be ready for an amazing evening."

Torie smiled as she watched her two friends. The fact that they were experiencing so much joy over a yearly event that she had come to dread, told her she still had some baggage to unpack over her own ideas around age. She might not like marking the passage of time, but she couldn't imagine not having that day to dread.

She caught Jasmin giving her a questioning look out of

the corner of her eye, but before she could say anything, she saw the front door to the bakery swing open as Max entered the building. He scanned the room before setting his dark eyes on the three women and then made his way over to them.

"Hi, Max," said Jasmin. "Please tell us you found out what happened with the mayor."

He shifted his weight from one leg to the other before reaching into his pocket.

"I did find something, just not sure what it means."

He withdrew a folded piece of paper and placed it on the coffee table in front of them.

Written on the paper in red ink was a single name, and underneath that, a phone number.

The name was Torie Bliss; underneath was her cell phone number and address.

"Would you happen to know why the dead mayor of Singing Falls had your name and contact information in his pocket, Torie?"

Grab your copy...
vinci-books.com/hexchocolate

About the Author

M.J. Caan is an avid reader and writer of all things science fiction and fantasy. Author of multiple science fiction and paranormal fantasy series, M.J. likes to think that there is still magic out there in the world. Even if it's only between the pages of a great book.